NANCY DREW
GHOST STORIES

$$\boxed{2}$$

NANCY DREW®
GHOST STORIES

2

by Carolyn Keene

Illustrated by Paul Frame

WANDERER BOOKS
Published by Simon & Schuster, Inc., New York

Published by WANDERER BOOKS
A Division of Simon & Schuster, Inc.
Simon & Schuster Building
1230 Avenue of the Americas
New York, New York 10020

Designed by Stanley S. Drate/Folio Graphics Co., Inc.

Manufactured in the United States of America

10 9 8 7 6 5 4 3 2

WANDERER and colophon are registered trademarks
of Simon & Schuster, Inc.

NANCY DREW is a trademark of Simon & Schuster, Inc.,
registered in the United States Patent and Trademark Office.

Library of Congress Cataloging in Publication Data

Keene, Carolyn.
  Nancy Drew ghost stories 2.

  Summary: Presents six adventures that involve Nancy
Drew and her friends with vampires, ghosts, witches, and
other evil and spooky characters.
  1. Detective and mystery stories, American.
2. Children's stories, American. [1. Mystery and
detective stories. 2. Ghosts—Fiction. 3. Short stories]
I. Frame, Paul, 1913-   ill. II. Title. III. Title:
Nancy Drew ghost stories two.
PZ7.K23Namc   1985   [Fic]   84-27045
ISBN 0-671-55075-6
ISBN 0-671-55070-5 (pbk.)

FOREWORD

Dear Readers,

When I thought about creating a collection of ghost stories, I knew that Nancy Drew would face her most intriguing challenge yet as a young detective. You see, Nancy does not believe in ghosts; but the many unexplained happenings in each mystery almost lead her to think otherwise.

Well, I won't spoil the fun by telling you about Nancy's amazing discoveries. You'll have to read the stories to find out what they are!

Carolyn Keene

CONTENTS

VAMPIRE
CAVE

A light, pearly mist was descending over the Allegheny Mountains as darkness fell. Nancy Drew looked out the living room window of the inn at which she and her friends Bess Marvin and George Fayne were staying. It was perched on the side of a hill, and she strained her eyes to spot the entrance to Craggy Cave.

"The mountains are beautiful, but they look spooky in this light," she observed.

"Wait till you get inside the cave," said tall, athletic George, who had suggested the girls stop off at the inn to go exploring. "It'll have underground streams, crystal caverns, *and it's haunted by ghosts,* according to Jenny."

"Ah, yes, it sure is," Jenny Shipton confirmed. She was the owner of the inn, an old, bent woman, but remarkably spry on her feet.

11

"Tell us about it!" Nancy said.

Bess Marvin, who was George's cousin, shivered. "I don't know if I want to hear this," she declared, shaking her fluffy blond hair.

"Oh, I do!" George said eagerly. Contrary to Bess, she was a tomboy and not afraid of anything.

"There's more in Craggy Cave than ghosts," Jenny warned. "If you want to go spelunking, go somewhere else. Not there!"

"Oh, come on," Nancy said. "It can't be that bad." She glanced at the old woman and noticed, to her surprise, that Jenny actually looked scared.

"The cave is full of bats," the innkeeper went on.

"Bats!" Bess cried, horrified. "That does it. I'm not going."

Jenny nodded her gray head. "Yes, bats. And worse than that. Long time ago, when folks was feudin' something awful around here in the hills, a man on the run hid in Craggy Cave. Never been heard of since. They say he was bitten by a bat and turned into a vampire!"

"You don't really believe that, Jenny, do you?" Nancy asked.

The old woman did not answer. "When the drums beat in Craggy Cave," she continued, "the vampire is on the prowl." Her voice was low and hoarse. "He attacks people!"

"But there's no such thing as a vampire!" Nancy protested.

"Don't tell *me*!" Jenny exclaimed. "I've seen him. His hair is black as coal, his face is white like the snow. He has evil black eyes that bore into your soul, and

12

long white fangs that he sinks into anyone who comes his way!"

Bess stuck her fingers into her ears. "I don't want to listen to this. Now I won't be able to sleep all night!"

Jenny looked at Nancy. "He wears black from head to toe," she whispered. "But his cloak is lined in red. Don't go near him. Don't go near Craggy Cave!"

"I think we should talk about this in the morning," George said. "I'm sure in the daylight things will look different."

Nancy agreed. "It's time we went to bed," she announced. "We have a busy day ahead."

As she spoke, a booming noise reverberated through the mountains. The effect on Jenny Shipton was startling. "It's the vampire!" she cried, shaking with fright.

"No, it's not," Nancy assured her gently. "It's just a thunderclap." As if to confirm her words, rain suddenly began to beat loudly on the roof.

The girls said goodnight to their hostess and went into their room. Bess spent a restless night. She tossed and turned.

"It was awful," she told her friends at breakfast. "I dreamed I was being chased by a vampire. And he looked just like Dracula!"

Yet, in the sparkling light of the morning, Jenny's tale of the vampire seemed less eerie and George began to plan the expedition.

"Let's not forget how easy it is to get lost in a cave," she reminded her companions. "Caves are like mazes, with tunnels going off in all directions."

"You're right," Nancy agreed. "And there are deep

13

sink holes. If you fall into one of those, and there's no one to help you out, you've had it!"

Bess looked unhappy. "I know the spelunking trip was one of the reasons we came here," she spoke up. "But do we have to go through with it?"

"Where's your sense of adventure, Bess?" Nancy teased. "Remember, Mr. Evans said there's some real exploring to do, especially in Craggy Cave."

Bess remained unconvinced. "There are other caverns in the area. Why don't we pick one of them? I don't want to see where the vampire lives."

"What vampire?" George grinned. "Now, before we do anything, we'll have to buy the necessary 'spelunk junk.' "

Bess groaned.

"We need nylon rope," George went on, "hard hats with flashlights built in, batteries, regular flashlights and—" she winked at Nancy—"survival rations for Bess." She knew she could usually mollify her cousin with the mention of food, which Bess was extremely fond of.

"You can buy all that stuff in Morton Bluff," Jenny Shipton said, pouring herself another cup of coffee. "Young fellow by the name of Ron Parker runs a store in town. He sells sports equipment and gift items. He's also my nearest neighbor. If I can catch him on the phone, maybe he'll give you a ride into town."

She made the call, and ten minutes later Ron Parker, a tall, blond young man in his late twenties, rolled up in his dusty old jeep. When they set out for Morton Bluff, the girls queried him about Craggy Cave.

Vampire Cave

Ron laughed when Bess mentioned the vampire. "Old wives' tales," he commented. "Nothing to them."

"Jenny Shipton claims she's seen the vampire," Bess insisted.

Ron made a face. "She's seeing things in her imagination, as she often does, living up there by herself near Craggy Cave. When are you planning to explore the place?"

"This afternoon," George said. "First we'd like to visit Evans Mansion."

"It's not open to visitors," Ron said. "The owner is in Europe."

"We know," Nancy told him. "But Mr. Evans is a friend of my father's and he said we can get the key from the bank president and see his paintings."

Ebenezer Evans, who was a millionaire, had one of the best private collections of primitive paintings, and the girls were very interested in seeing them.

Ron Parker looked surprised. "You really think they'll let you in?" he asked.

"Sure," Nancy replied. "We're to pick the key up from Mr. Knox. He's expecting us this morning. Can you drop us off there? Later we'll come to your store and get our spelunk junk."

Ron smiled. "I'll be glad to. Matter of fact, I'll drive you to the mansion. I haven't seen the paintings, either, and I'd like to come with you. My partner Jim is at the store, so I can take some time off."

Soon the group arrived at the bank and spoke to a clerk named Henry Smith. He was a small, wizened man with an air of perpetual worry. He announced the

15

visitors to Mr. Knox over the intercom, then ushered them into the banker's private office.

Mr. Knox stood up and extended his hand. "I'm glad to meet you girls. Hi, Ron. Have you been elected as the Drew party's special tour guide?"

Ron grinned. "I gave them a lift into town. Do you mind if I go along to see the mansion? I haven't been inside myself yet."

"No, go right ahead," Mr. Knox said. "Mr. Smith will come along, too, and turn off the alarm. We know we can trust you people. When you're through, just lock the door. That automatically reactivates the security system. Then you can bring the key back."

The girls thanked the bank president and the group walked outside. Mr. Smith squeezed into the back seat of the jeep with George and Bess. "I'll walk back from the mansion," he said. "It's not far."

Soon the jeep rolled through the impressive gate of the Evans Mansion, which lay on the outskirts of the small town toward Craggy Cave. Ron parked and everyone climbed out. Mr. Smith unlocked the heavy oak door, then deactivated the alarm. He handed the key to Nancy. "Enjoy yourselves," he said. "Mr. Evans has a real treasure here for art lovers. Take your time."

"Thanks," Nancy said and waved good-bye. She went inside, followed by Ron and her friends. Their footsteps echoed eerily on the marble floor of the huge entrance hall.

"It's beautiful!" Bess breathed as they walked into the ornate living room. She admired the antique furniture as well as the rare paintings.

Now and then, the girls noticed an empty spot on the walls. "Mr. Evans must have sold several of his pictures," Nancy said.

George nodded. "I wonder if there are any others in the study," she said and went off to look while Bess and Nancy examined a heavy, carved table, whose top was inlaid with different kinds of wood, forming an intricate design.

Ron trailed after George into the study. She stood before the painting of a woman in a garden, which hung over the fireplace, and admired the striking colors. When she finally turned, her eyes caught a folded piece of paper on the floor. She picked it up and looked at it.

"What is it?" Ron asked curiously, glancing over her shoulder.

"A handwritten list of paintings," George replied. "Mr. Evans must have made this."

Her gaze was drawn to another picture and she walked over to it, absentmindedly putting the crumpled list into her pocket. "Look at this beautiful portrait!" she exclaimed. "The eyes of that woman are absolutely haunting!"

"They are," Ron agreed. "Well, I'd better be going now. I want to make sure that Jim's minding the store. See you girls later. I'll give you a ride to the cave, if you want."

"That'll be great," George said. Then she turned to the portrait once more. Soon she heard the noise of the jeep's engine, as it rattled down the driveway.

Nancy and Bess were studying a fine collection of

17

old swords displayed in the hall, when George strolled into the next room, a huge library. She examined the paintings there. Then she went to a door which she thought would lead to an adjoining room. An ornate key was in the lock, but she did not have to turn it to open the door.

George chuckled. She was looking into a large, empty closet! She was about to close the door again when she heard a footstep behind her. She started to move her head when a pair of hands struck her sharply in the back. She plunged into the closet, bumping her head on the rear wall!

The door slammed shut behind her. George picked herself up, anger welling up inside her. She tried the door, but it was locked. Loudly she yelled for her companions. They didn't hear her.

This is crazy, George thought. *Someone else is in the house with us. But who? Ron's gone, I heard his car drive away. Did he leave the front door open by any chance?*

She banged her fists on the door. "Nancy! Bess!" she shouted.

There was no response.

Nancy and Bess had gone to the second floor and were exploring the beautifully decorated bedrooms. Finally they had seen enough.

"Time to go," Nancy decided. "Let's get on with our next project."

"Where's George?" Bess wondered. "She hasn't been with us for quite a while."

"That's right," Nancy said. "Do you think she left

with Ron?"

"I doubt it," Bess said. "She would have told us."

"Let's look for her," Nancy suggested. "I'll search all the rooms up here, you go check downstairs."

Bess went to the first floor and made her way through the house. After a while, a faint rhythmic pounding reached her ears from the direction of the library.

She ran back to the bottom of the stairs. "Nancy!" she cried out. "Come down here!"

A moment later, both girls hurried to the source of the noise. They found the closet door and turned the knob. It would not budge.

"George, are you in there?" Nancy cried.

"Yes. Please open up."

"Wait a minute. There's no key." Nancy pulled her miniature detective kit out of her purse and removed several small tools. She picked at the lock until she felt it turn. A second later she opened the door and George stumbled out.

"Boy, am I glad to see you!" she gasped. "Someone must be in the house with us," she added with a shudder. "Do you think we should go looking for him?"

Nancy shook her head. "This place is huge, and he probably knows all the hiding places. We'd better hurry back to Mr. Knox and tell him what happened."

Bess nodded vigorously. "Yes, let's get out of here fast, or that creep'll catch all of us!"

The girls ran to the door and Nancy pulled out the key Mr. Smith had given her. "This will activate the alarm," she said. "Unless the intruder knows the system, he'll be in trouble when he tries to leave."

George was already running down the steps. Suddenly, out of the corner of her eye, she noticed a shadow on the roof of the mansion. She looked up and saw a large block of plaster come loose from a cornice.

It hurtled directly at her!

Instinctively, George jumped out of the way. The heavy plaster hit the ground with terrific force and broke into many pieces.

"Somebody's on the roof!" George cried out.

At the same moment, the girls heard footsteps heading across the roof toward the back. Without a word, they ran to the rear of the house. A wing jutted out in front of them and they had to go around it. When they finally reached the back, they saw a tall ash right next to the house. A man was shinnying down the tree, covered by the dense foliage. A moment later he dove into the bushes.

The girls chased him, but soon lost his trail as he disappeared into the woods of the huge estate.

"One thing's for sure," Nancy panted. "He knows his way around here, inside and outside the house."

George nodded grimly. "He must have gone upstairs by another stairway when you and Bess were coming down. Then he climbed out a window into the tree before we put the alarm back on."

"But why would he want to harm you?" Bess asked her cousin worriedly.

"I have no idea." George looked puzzled.

"First he pushed you into the closet, then he tried to finish you off with that block of plaster," Nancy said. "It doesn't make sense."

"Perhaps he picked me because I was in the right spot for him," George reasoned. "Any one of us might have served his purpose. Apparently, he wanted to chase us away from this place."

Bess nodded. "Let's tell Mr. Knox, and the police, too."

The girls walked back to the bank. Just before they reached the building, they saw Mr. Smith in front of them. He seemed in a hurry and ducked through the door.

"That's strange," George said. "He should have been back long before now."

"Maybe he was, but went out again on an errand," Bess suggested.

Nancy nodded. "It's possible. But he acted rather strangely, as if he didn't want anyone to see him. We should keep an eye on this man."

"Shall we tell Mr. Knox about him?" George wanted to know.

"No," Nancy decided. "We have no proof that Mr. Smith did anything wrong. But we'll report everything that happened at the mansion."

The banker was shocked when he heard the girls' story and called the police right away. "They must search the place thoroughly," he added. "Mr. Evans would be furious if a burglar got into his house and stole his priceless possessions. Now, you better be careful; and if you run into anything unusual, call me at once."

"We will," Nancy promised.

Fifteen minutes later, the trio reached Ron Parker's store. It was large and crammed with all kinds of sports equipment, gift items, and party goods, including Halloween costumes. Jim showed them things they would need for spelunking. They amused themselves by trying on hard hats, each choosing a different color, as they waited for Ron, who was serving a customer in the gift department.

When he had finished and the girls had made their purchases, they all climbed into his jeep. Nancy and Bess slid into the back while George sat next to Ron.

He drove through the small town and into the hills. On the way, he asked the girls if they had enjoyed their visit to the Evans Mansion. When he heard about the incidents, he was shocked.

"George, whoever did that was purposely trying to harm you!" he exploded. "He should be in jail! I hope the police find out who he is."

Ron was so agitated that he almost missed a turn. He yanked the wheel sharply to the left at the last moment, and the jeep shot over the rocky road. The sudden move caused the door on the passenger side to fly open. Carried by the car's momentum, George pitched out of her seat!

Nancy lunged forward and managed to grasp her friend's shirt in the nick of time. With a grunt, she pulled George back into the jeep.

Ron jammed on the brakes. When the car had stopped, he jumped out and examined the door.

"Someone tampered with the catch!" he fumed. "I wonder if it was the same man who was after you girls at the mansion!"

"Possibly," Nancy said. "But how did he know we'd be driving with you?"

"He must have seen us come into town together this morning," Ron reasoned. "So he figured I'd give you a ride home, too."

"We'd better make sure he isn't following us!" George spoke up. "I wouldn't want to encounter him in the cave."

Ron looked in the rearview mirror. "I don't see anyone," he said. "But I'll do a little fancy driving anyway, just to be sure."

He made several quick turns, backtracking in the process, and did not head for Craggy Cave until he was convinced no one was behind them.

"When you get into Crystal Cavern," he advised the girls, "you'll come to a place where there are three tunnels close together. Follow the one on the left, and you'll find a second opening. Not many people know about it, but just in case you have a problem, you'll know there's another way out."

"Thanks," Bess said. "I'm not even sure I want to go in!"

George chuckled. "After what happened to me at the Evans Mansion, Craggy Cave will be an easy trip."

Ron pulled up in front of the cavern entrance and the girls climbed out of the jeep. Nancy carried their neatly coiled rope on her shoulder, while George toted the flashlights. Bess had a supply of food in a plastic bag, and each of the three wore a brightly colored hard hat.

Ron waved and drove off. The young detectives entered the cave. The huge crystal cavern was wired for lights, and they gasped in admiration whey they stepped into the underground wonderland of towering limestone stalagmites, the crags that gave the cave its name. Above them was a dense ceiling of stalactites that dropped like pendants from a vast chandelier.

"Stalagmites and stalactites," Bess mused. "It's hard to remember which is which."

" 'G' is on the ground, 'c' is on the ceiling," Nancy informed her.

The threesome left the lighted cavern and struck off down the tunnel on the left that Ron had told them about.

As darkness enveloped them, they switched on the lights of their hard hats. The tunnel grew smaller and smaller, and soon it became nothing but a crawl space.

"Oh, no!" Bess muttered. "Ron didn't warn us about this."

Cautiously, Nancy eased herself through the low gap in the rock. "It's okay," she said after a minute. "We're coming into another cave."

George was right behind her. Bess followed bravely, but suddenly her plump form became wedged in the crawl space. "Help me, I'm stuck!" she squealed.

"Don't worry, we'll get you out," George shouted. She turned around and instructed her cousin to stretch out and inch along. At the same time, she grasped Bess's hand and pulled her through.

"I hope we don't have to go back that way," Bess complained when she got to her feet.

The girls could hear water running in the darkness ahead. Nancy beamed her flashlight in that direction and saw an underground stream cutting through the cave.

"I wonder what's on the other side," she said and walked up to the stream. It seemed quite shallow and she stepped right into it. However, the water was deeper than she had anticipated, and the treacherous current caught her off balance. She fell headlong into the swiftly running stream! Her flashlight was torn from her hand and she was swept away, helplessly bobbing in the middle of the stream.

"George!" Bess cried in a trembling voice. "Do you hear that water roaring over a cliff? There's an underground waterfall ahead. If we don't do something, Nancy will drown!"

The cousins rushed along the edge of the stream. Soon they felt the spray coming from the fall. George played her flashlight along the ground. She saw a rock, or crag, jutting out at the edge of the stream just before it emptied into a boiling cauldron.

"Hold onto me, Bess!" she cried, crawling onto the rock. "It will help steady me."

With Bess tugging on her jeans, she reached out and grabbed Nancy's hand, yanking her friend out of the water just as she was about to disappear into the cauldron.

Nancy was shivering with cold as she collapsed on the cavern floor. "Thanks, girls," she panted. "You just saved my life!"

"Let's get out of this place," Bess urged. "It's too dangerous."

Nancy nodded. "But only long enough for me to change my clothes!"

"I see a tunnel on this side of the stream," George said. "Maybe it leads to the exit Ron told us about. If it does, it'll be quicker than retracing our steps."

"If only it weren't so dark," Bess complained as they

pressed on. "We can't really see what kind of passage we're in. I'd rather—"

She stopped short and gasped. "Did you hear that?" she whispered.

George and Nancy stood still and listened. From up ahead came a whirring sound that seemed to be growing in intensity.

"It's a drum!" Bess cried. "Jenny Shipton mentioned it when she told us about the vampire!"

The girls stared at one another in the dim light of their headgear, uncertain what to do.

"Let's go on," Nancy decided finally. "We have to find the exit. Besides, we know vampires don't exist, don't we?"

"I'm not sure," Bess murmured, but bravely followed her friend.

A few steps farther on, they entered yet another cavern. The strange whirring came from above, and George beamed her flashlight to the ceiling.

The girls shrieked! Hundreds of bats were flying from the roof of the cave, to which they had been clinging, in a solid mass, like an army. The whirring sound was caused by their wings, echoing from the walls of the underground structure.

The bats headed into a large tunnel opposite the girls.

"That's good," Nancy said in relief. "They're flying out to feed. That means there has to be an exit at the end of this tunnel."

"It's a good thing they didn't come our way," George said. "We'd have been in real danger!"

Vampire Cave

Bess moaned at the mere thought. The girls waited until the bats had vanished, then started down the tunnel. George was in the lead, with Nancy and Bess right behind her. Suddenly Bess tripped and fell. Nancy turned around to help her friend up.

"Are you okay?" she asked.

Bess nodded. "Yes. Just don't go so fast."

Nancy took her by the hand. George was quite a distance ahead of them by now. Suddenly a rock bounced off a ledge on the side of the tunnel and landed with a thud right in front of her. Startled, she beamed her flashlight upwards.

Then she let out a piercing scream!

On the ledge, hovered a weird creature. It had black hair, black eyes, a face as white as snow, and long white fangs protruding from its mouth! Wrapped in a long, black cape with red lining, it stood silently, watching the girl.

Before the petrified detective could make another move, the vampire suddenly shot forward. With a loud grunt and outstretched arms it swooped down in a great leap, the sides of its cape spread out like two huge, red wings. It seized George by the wrist and dragged her off through the tunnel.

The girl screamed and struggled while Nancy and Bess dashed to catch up. "Help!" George cried. "Help me! He—"

Suddenly the sound was cut off.

"George, where are you?" Nancy yelled.

There was no answer.

Nancy and Bess ran around the next bend, playing

27

their flashlights ahead of them.

"Listen!" Nancy whispered.

By straining their ears, the two could hear the faint echo of George's voice ahead of them. They rushed forward. Suddenly Nancy stopped short and grabbed Bess's arm.

"There's a sinkhole!" she cried.

A vast opening in the floor of the cave yawned in front of them. Another step and they would have fallen over the edge!

George's voice rose eerily from its depth. Peering down, Nancy and Bess saw her clinging desperately to a piece of rock jutting out from the side of the hole. The outcropping had broken her fall to the bottom, which was too far down for anyone to see!

Quickly, Nancy lowered her rope. George grabbed it, and with combined effort, Bess and Nancy pulled her out.

"The vampire threw me in!" the girl gasped as she lay exhausted on the ground, recovering her breath. "Then he ran off around the side of the hole. It was horrible. Those fangs and those huge red wings! Why did he come after me like that?"

"We'll find out," Nancy declared grimly, hugging her friend. "We all know he wasn't a real vampire. Now, let's get to that exit. I see light at the end of the tunnel. We can't be far."

"Be careful," Bess warned. "Maybe he's waiting for us outside."

The girls were silent and scared as they cautiously made their way to the opening. However, no one was there. The sun shone down warmly on them, and birds could be heard singing in the trees.

Quickly, they ran to Jenny Shipton's inn. The old woman stared at Nancy when they arrived. "Ye're wet as a fish!" she said. "Took a dunking, did ye?"

"I fell into a stream in Craggy Cave," Nancy explained.

Jenny's eyebrows shot up. "So you did go there after all!"

George nodded. "And we saw the vampire."

Jenny gave her a sharp look. "I warned ye," was all she said.

When George took off her dirty jeans, she suddenly remembered the piece of paper she had picked up at the Evans Mansion. She pulled it out of her pocket.

"That's strange!" she said. "It's torn. And it wasn't before. I had the whole thing, now I only have a little piece of it!"

"What was it?" Nancy asked curiously.

"A list of paintings Mr. Evans must have made. I found it by the fireplace in the study. I showed it to Ron, but he didn't know what it was for, either."

Nancy studied the scrap of paper. 'Henry Rousseau—The' were the only words on it.

She shrugged and gave it back to George. "Hold onto this," she advised. "It may be a clue."

She put on a dry pair of shoes. "Let's go back to Mr. Knox and tell him what happened," she suggested.

A half hour later, the young detectives approached the bank. Nancy saw Ron Parker pull up and go inside. She stopped suddenly, her forehead creased in a frown.

"I have an idea," she said. "You two go into the bank. Get Ron into Mr. Knox's office and tell them what

30

happened. I'll join you in about fifteen minutes. Don't let anyone leave until I get there, okay?"

Bess and George nodded. They knew better than to ask questions when they saw that look on Nancy's face. A moment later they entered the bank and walked up to Henry Smith's desk. He led them into the president's office, then went to get Ron Parker. When they were all assembled, George and Bess took turns explaining what had happened to them in Craggy Cave.

George acted out the scene where the vampire had swooped down from the ledge and grabbed her, and Bess shivered all over again when she remembered the danger they had been in.

"This is incredible!" Mr. Knox cried out. "Where's Nancy?"

"She'll be here shortly," George said. "She said for all of us to wait for her."

Ron was outraged. "I can't imagine why anyone would do something like that!" he stormed. "You girls shouldn't even walk around the street without a police escort!"

As he was speaking, the door opened slightly. A vampire face peered around its edge!

The banker and his clerk gasped, and the two girls retreated behind Mr. Knox's desk, shrieking. Just then the unsavory creature stuck its thumb under its chin and, with a jerk, pulled off the mask.

"Nancy!" George cried out.

Ron had turned pale. He began to move toward the door, but the police chief, who was right behind Nancy, stopped him from leaving the room.

"I had a little trouble getting the mask from Jim,"

Nancy said. "I told him Ron had asked me to bring it over here. He found it in Ron's desk."

Mr. Knox stared at the girl. "Nancy, I'm not sure I like this masquerade. You scared us half to death!"

"I figured out the game Ron has been playing," the girl went on. "Parts I can only guess, but I suppose the police will find out whether I'm right or not."

"I don't know what you're talking about!" Ron protested. "I haven't been playing any game . . ."

"No. It was more than that," Nancy agreed. "You almost killed George!"

"That's preposterous!" Ron cried out. "What possible reason could I have for doing that?"

"She found the list of paintings you made and lost in the Evans Mansion. You probably dropped it when you stole the pictures that account for the bare spots on the walls!"

Mr. Knox stared at Ron, who laughed derisively. "That's ridiculous," the shopkeeper said. "I couldn't get into that place, and neither could anyone else. The alarm system is foolproof."

"That's true," Nancy said. "But you found a secret passage from Craggy Cave to the mansion. It ended at the fireplace in the study, didn't it? When you had access to the house, you made a list of all the paintings, then contacted dealers who would buy certain ones."

She paused a moment, then continued. "Once you had your order, you went in and stole the pictures. But you dropped the list by mistake on your way out. When George picked it up, you were afraid she'd show it to someone who would recognize your handwriting. So you went after her."

"That's why you pushed me into the closet!" George spoke up.

"Nonsense," Ron said. "I left before that happened."

"But you went back after parking your car down the road," Henry Smith spoke up.

All eyes turned to him.

"I stayed a while to see what you were up to, but finally I had to leave or Mr. Knox would have wondered where I was," the clerk went on.

"You didn't manage to get the list out of my pocket when you pushed me," George took up the story again, "so you loosened the plaster on the roof when we left. You figured it would hit me and you could come to my aid, retrieving the list in the process of helping me."

"And when that didn't work," Bess put in, "you made that sudden turn in the road. You knew the door on the passenger side wasn't locked properly. If George fell out, you'd have another chance to get close to her and reach into her pocket."

"It's a fascinating story, but pure fabrication," Ron said coolly.

Nancy was undaunted by his comment. "You dropped us off at the cave and told us where to go so you could play vampire," she went on. "You managed to get George and throw her into the sink hole. At that point, you retrieved the list, but it tore. She still has enough of it to prove that it was in your handwriting!"

Ron's jaw sagged, as George pulled out the piece of paper and handed it to Mr. Knox.

"We have samples of Ron's writing here at the bank," he said. "It'll be easy enough to compare this with them."

Ron collapsed into the nearest chair. He knew he had lost. Bess turned to him. "I have one question," she said. "You must have been playing vampire before this. Jenny Shipton swears she saw a creature that looked exactly like you."

Ron shrugged. "I may as well tell you," he said. "My uncle told me just before he died that there was an access route to the mansion from Craggy Cave. I spent hours and hours looking for it. When people appeared, I scared them away with my vampire act. I couldn't risk being seen there time and again. Soon no one came around, until you showed up."

"Why did you accompany us to the mansion?" Bess went on.

"I was afraid you might tell Mr. Knox about the missing paintings," Ron confessed. "When I heard you guess that Mr. Evans had sold them, my mind was put at ease, and I figured I'd be able to continue my racket until Evans came back from Europe."

"Well, it's all over now," Mr. Knox said. "You'll go to jail not only for theft, but for assault, too."

"And Craggy Cave will once again become the tourist attraction it used to be," Mr. Smith smiled.

"I bet there's one person in town who'll be disappointed!" George said.

"Who's that?" Mr. Knox asked, looking surprised.

"Jenny Shipton. She won't like to hear that the vampire she believed in was her neighbor!"

THE DARK CRYPT

Nancy Drew maneuvered her blue sports sedan through the River Heights traffic and headed into the countryside.

"As I told you on the phone, Mrs. Campbell has a mystery for us," she told her friends Bess Marvin and George Fayne, who were in the back seat. "It involves a ghost."

"You didn't say anything about a ghost!" blonde Bess protested. "I wouldn't have come along if I had known that!"

Her cousin George, a slender, athletic girl who did not scare as easily as Bess, chuckled. "That's why Nancy didn't tell you!"

Bess bit her lip. "Where does Mrs. Campbell live?" she asked. "And how did you meet her, Nancy?"

"My Dad did some legal work for Mrs. Campbell," Nancy replied. "She lives a few miles out of town, is about sixty years old, and all she told Dad is that she needs help with a ghost."

Bess rolled her eyes upward. "Just what I need. Why—" Suddenly, she let out a frightened yell. "Duck!"

Before Nancy and George could react, a rock hit the top of the car and slid through the open sun roof into the blue sedan. It landed on George's lap!

Startled, Nancy hit the brakes and pulled to the side of the road. "What in the world was that!" she cried.

George held up the stone. It had a piece of paper wrapped around it. "A strange way to deliver mail!" she fumed. She removed the rubber band that held the note in place, then unfolded the paper.

" 'Go back to River Heights or I'll finish you off!' " she read aloud.

Bess stared at the crudely scrawled letters. "I don't like this one bit!" she declared. "Maybe we should turn around."

"No way!" her cousin said firmly. "Whoever threw that note into our car isn't going to scare us, right, Nancy?"

The titian-haired detective agreed. "Let's get out and see if we find a clue to who wants to prevent us from seeing Mrs. Campbell," she suggested.

The girls climbed out of the car. Bess was reluctant, but followed without saying another word. They ran into the bushes, where they heard twigs snapping ahead of them.

"There he is!" Nancy cried. "Come on!"

They plunged deeper into the underbrush, but the going was slow because of the thick foliage. Suddenly, they heard a motor roar to life. A car started up, then the noise grew faint and died away in the distance.

"He was prepared for a quick getaway," Nancy said in disappointment as they made their way back to the road.

Just then, George bent down and picked something up from the ground. "Look at this!" she exclaimed.

"A slingshot!" Bess said, after examining the object. "The man fired the stone from a slingshot! If it was a man," she added.

George nodded. "It could have been a woman. We don't know yet."

"I really have no great desire to find out," Bess muttered.

Nancy put an arm around her friend. "Oh, come on. We've had worse things happen to us before."

"That's true," Bess admitted. Then she laughed. "All right, let's go see Mrs. Campbell!"

Half an hour later, the girls turned into a long driveway leading to a large, white-framed house with black shutters. It was quite a distance from the road and hidden by a clump of trees. A red barn stood off to one side, and a duck pond, fringed with waterlilies, stretched out in front.

"An old-fashioned farmhouse!" Bess cried. "It's very pretty!"

Mrs. Campbell, a chubby woman with curly, gray hair, greeted the girls at the door and ushered them onto her back porch. "I'm so glad you came," she said. "Please sit down. I have some lemonade and snacks ready for you in the kitchen. Make yourselves comfortable while I get them."

Bess's eyes lit up. She loved to eat, and when she bit

into a homemade piece of pecan pie a few minutes later, she was as eager to hear about the mystery as George and Nancy.

"It all happened ten years ago," Mrs. Campbell began. "That's when my husband inherited this house from his father and we moved from our apartment in River Heights. We had some valuable heirlooms, and the moving company foreman, Mr. Becker, drove them in his own car."

"What kind of heirlooms?" Bess inquired.

"We had a Paul Revere silver tea service, a priceless heirloom, and flatware crafted by Hester Bateman, the great English silversmith of the eighteenth century. Things like that."

"Oh, I'd love to see them!" George exclaimed.

"They're gone," Mrs. Campbell said sadly. "Mr. Becker was hijacked on the way over here. The hijackers took them from his car, put them in their van and got away."

"Maybe he stole them himself!" George spoke up.

"Nobody knows," Mrs. Campbell replied. "The police were suspicious and got his fingerprints. When they checked their records, they found he was wanted for armed robbery!

"This was another case, though," Mrs. Campbell continued, "not ours! Becker has been in prison ever since, convicted of that crime. But he never admitted he took our heirlooms, and we have never recovered them."

"You mentioned a ghost when you spoke to my dad," Nancy put in. "Can you tell us about that?"

Mrs. Campbell took a faded envelope from the pocket of her jacket and handed it to the girl. Inside was a note, printed in blue crayon.

" 'Ghost guards treasure where entrance leads to darkness,' " Nancy read. "What does this mean?"

"I have no idea. I found it when I was tidying the attic. It was on the floor under an old trunk that had not been moved since we got here. I have a feeling that the treasure mentioned in this letter refers to our heirlooms. But I can't figure out where the ghost is that guards an entrance leading into darkness."

"Becker could have dropped this note," Nancy reasoned. "Maybe he hid the heirlooms, then reported them stolen. He could have written the note for an accomplice, but dropped it by mistake."

Mrs. Campbell nodded. "That's what I thought. But do you have any—" She stopped when Nancy suddenly jumped up and rushed across the porch. The young detective had spotted a furtive figure in the hedge, spying on them! She hurried to the spot, but the eavesdropper had already dashed across the backyard next door and ducked into the woods.

Nancy followed, but soon lost his trail and returned to the porch.

"Someone else was anxious to hear about your mystery," she told Mrs. Campbell. "Too bad he got away before I could see what he looked like."

"Do you think he overheard our conversation?" Bess asked worriedly.

Nancy shook her head. "No. He was too far away. But I bet that's what he came for!" She thought of the incident on the road but did not mention it to their hostess. She did not want to further upset the woman.

Mrs. Campbell stood up. "That hedge divides my property from my neighbor's, Mr. Hansen," she declared. "I'd better let him know there was a prowler around."

"If we're lucky, Mr. Hansen was looking out the window just now and saw more of that man than I did," Nancy said hopefully.

A few minutes after Mrs. Campbell called her neighbor, a stocky man with beady brown eyes and an impressive black mustache came over from the house next door. "I'm George Hansen," he introduced himself to the girls as he walked up the steps. He shook hands with everyone, a friendly smile on his face.

"I thought I'd come over and talk to you," he went on. "I'm worried about that prowler. I wonder what he could have been after."

Nancy shrugged. "Did you happen to see him, Mr. Hansen?"

The man shook his head. "No. But I bet this has something to do with Mrs. Campbell's mystery."

Nancy was surprised to hear that the woman had told anyone else about her problem, but did not comment. Instead, she turned to her hostess. "Would you mind if we look around the house a bit?" she inquired. "Perhaps we'll find another clue."

"Oh, no, go right ahead," Mrs. Campbell said, then poured a glass of lemonade for Mr. Hansen.

The young detectives excused themselves and began

a systematic search of the house. They inspected the attic, a huge, dusty area with boxes and suitcases piled high in one corner. Then they worked their way through every room until they ended up in the basement. There they found a cluttered assortment of old furniture and appliances. None of it seemed to have been touched in years.

The girls sighed and set to work, shifting all the pieces and looking for anything that might give them an idea of where the heirlooms could be.

"I'm going to lose five pounds doing all this heavy work!" Bess said, rubbing her forehead and spreading the dust into her blonde hair.

"That'll be terrific!" George quipped, glancing at her cousin's plump figure. "Only trouble is, you'll gain it all back at dinner time!"

Bess made a face. "Why don't you come over here and help me move this book case?" she said. "Nancy, you, too. This job will require all three of us."

When the girls managed to slide the heavy piece of furniture to one side, Bess noticed the outline of a rectangle about five-by-three feet in the cement floor underneath. There was an iron ring at one end of the panel. "A trapdoor!" she cried out. "Look!"

"You just made a great discovery," Nancy declared. She pulled on the ring, but it was stuck tight.

George saw a crowbar lying in one corner and picked it up. "Try this," she suggested.

Nancy pushed the crowbar through the ring. Slowly she pried up the metal panel and lifted it to one side. A flight of stone steps were leading into darkness!

43

"It's pitch black," Bess said. "We're not going down there, are we?"

Nancy pulled her pencil flashlight out of her pocket. "Yes, we are," she said. "Don't worry, I'll go first."

Cautiously, she descended step-by-step into the darkness below. The stairs were damp, and she struggled to keep her footing. Suddenly a hand reached out and clutched her shoulder!

With a muffled cry, Nancy spun around.

"It's only me," George gasped. "Sorry. I almost lost my balance."

At the bottom of the stone steps was a small room with brick walls. It was empty, and there was no other access besides the way they had come.

"I wonder what this was used for," Nancy said.

"Well, the heirlooms certainly aren't here," Bess declared.

"Neither is a ghost," George chuckled.

The words made Bess shiver. "Let's go back and ask Mrs. Campbell about this place," she said and was the first to hurry up the stairs.

Their hostess was still sitting on the porch talking to her neighbor. When the girls told her about the secret room they had found, she frowned. "I had no idea it was there," she said. "There are many stories about this old house. One has it that smugglers once used it. The ringleader was an ancestor of my husband. Maybe he built the room to hide his contraband, or his men."

"At first we thought the cryptic message you found referred to that room," George spoke up. "But I guess it was a false clue."

"Crypt," Nancy repeated thoughtfully. "Maybe that's

it! Mrs. Campbell, do you have a family crypt in the Bayport Cemetery?"

"Why, yes," the woman replied. "But it hasn't been opened in twenty years!"

"I wonder if your heirlooms could be hidden there," the girl speculated. "The word *ghost* could refer to the cemetery, and the *entrance leading to darkness* could be the door!"

"This is beginning to sound like a tale by Edgar Allan Poe!" Mrs. Campbell said with a smile. "But if you want to check it out, go right ahead."

She went into the kitchen and returned with a rusty old key. "The crypt is almost at the end, on the left," she said.

Bess took the key, looked at it curiously, then put it in her purse. "Come on," she said in an uncommon spurt of courage. "Let's see if we can find the treasure."

The three girls went out through the front door. Mr. Hansen, who had finished his lemonade, said good-bye to Mrs. Campbell and retraced his steps across his backyard.

George volunteered to drive this time, and Nancy sat next to her. She turned to Bess, who was in the back, and said, "Let me have a look at that key, will you?"

Bess pulled it out of her purse and handed it to Nancy. "It's really old," the young detective said. "It has *Campbell Crypt, River Heights Cemetery* embossed on it." After inspecting the key thoroughly, Nancy put it in her pocketbook. "It's getting dark," she observed. "I'm glad it's a clear night, and there's a full moon. At least we'll be able to find our way."

Bess began to regret having suggested that they go to

the cemetery, but she didn't say anything. By the time they arrived, the moon threw a silvery light through the trees. The mournful call of a night owl made the girls shiver. But they left their car at the entrance and bravely walked through the massive gate.

A chilly breeze had replaced the heat of the afternoon, and it wafted the scent of flowers in the girls' nostrils. The trees, swaying in the wind, took on grotesque shapes and towered like giant black spirits above the graves.

"This place isn't my idea of fun," Bess complained in a whisper. "Maybe we should come back tomorrow."

"No, it's easier to scout around now," Nancy said. "There are no people here who might get the wrong idea."

The marble crypts, each with its own quota of flowers and shrubs, gleamed silver as the moon rose higher. They were an eerie sight.

Cautiously, the friends walked down the center path. Every step they took on the gravel sounded loud in the spooky silence. Ghostlike statues, interspersed among the graves, seemed to move in the breeze.

Suddenly a sepulchral voice thundered through the cemetery. "Nancy Dreeeeeeew! Beware! I am a Campbell who has risen from the grave to warn you! Leave this cemetery at once or you will be in great danger!"

Nancy, Bess, and George stood stockstill, dumbfounded.

"N-Nancy, let's go!" Bess urged.

"No way!" the young detective replied. "This is no ghost, just someone trying to scare us."

"Well, he's succeeded," Bess declared. "I'm leaving."

"Okay, you go back to the car and wait for us," Nancy suggested. "If you see anything funny, honk the horn!"

Bess turned without another word and hurried away. Nancy and George pressed on. They were sure that the crypt was not far away. Suddenly George grabbed Nancy's hand. "Did you hear that?" she whispered.

"Yes. Someone tried to cry, but it was kind of muffled," Nancy agreed. "Maybe it was Bess. We'd better see if she's okay."

As the girls turned to retrace their steps, the sepulchral voice could be heard again. "Nancy Dreeeeew! Leave at once. Go, or you will not get out of here alive!"

"I'm getting worried," George said.

Nancy nodded. "Let's go to the car and see if Bess is there."

But when the girls arrived at Nancy's blue sedan, Bess Marvin was nowhere in sight.

"That muffled cry came from over there," Nancy said when the girls had returned to the center path. She took George's hand, and together the girls began to search for their friend.

"Bess?" George called out. "Bess, where are you?"

There was no reply.

A lump formed in Nancy's stomach. What had happened to Bess? Suddenly there was a slight movement behind a statue to their left. "George, over there!" Nancy hissed.

Cautiously, the girls walked toward the spot, their eyes riveted on the statue.

"Bess?" Nancy called out again.

Suddenly she felt something hitting her in the back, and she pitched forward. The next moment, she tumbled into a deep, black hole!

Out of the corner of her eye, George saw a dark figure, wearing a mask, push her friend. She realized that they were just at the edge of an open grave. Before the man could attack her, she lashed out with a well-aimed karate chop. He flew backward, and rolled over, then sprang to his feet again. With a grunt, he rushed at George, but she evaded him skillfully, poised for another strike.

The man realized he had an opponent whose agility he could not match. He managed to get out of George's way and ran toward the gate.

George turned and looked for her friend. "Nancy?" she cried out.

"Down here," Nancy replied.

George stared into the open grave. "Bess!" she exclaimed.

"That man gagged her and dumped her in this hole," Nancy explained. "Help pull her out." She hoisted the blonde girl up, and Bess, once she was safe, slumped down on the grass with a sigh. Nancy, meanwhile, found a foothold and, grasping George's hand tightly, managed to climb out of the empty grave.

"Whew!" she said. "Someone wants to keep us away from that crypt, that's for sure!"

Just then, the girls heard a car start in the distance. "He chickened out," Nancy said with a grin. "George, how'd you get him to run?"

"Karate," George said. "He was a bit on the heavy

side and not too agile, and I managed to flatten him. He wore a mask so we wouldn't recognize him. Maybe he figured it was better to run than to risk having his mask pulled off in a fight."

"Good work!" Nancy hugged her friend with glee.

"You're not continuing this search, are you?" Bess asked, getting up from the grass. "I'm in no shape to—"

"Sure you are," Nancy said. "The guy's gone. Now is the time. Come on, girls!"

Reluctantly, George and Bess followed Nancy to the Campbell crypt. It was a large structure, about twelve feet square and six feet high, with the family name carved on marble above the door.

Nancy took the key from her handbag, inserted it, and opened the door. It swung inward with an eerie creak.

She shined her light on the musty interior, and the girls stepped farther into the crypt. Marble slabs holding coffins lined the walls.

Nancy played the beam of her flashlight over them, then let it rest on a coffin that stood on the floor toward the left, underneath a marble slab. Its lid was slightly ajar!

"I don't see Mrs. Campbell's treasure," George whispered. "Only her relatives!"

"Wait a minute," Nancy said. "See that coffin on the floor? It has no name plate on it like the others. And its top isn't on tight!"

"You're not going to open that coffin!" Bess objected. "Are you out of your mind?"

But Nancy had already grabbed the coffin and pulled

it out from under the slab. She pushed up the lid, and the three girls stared in amazement. Inside the box were objects wrapped in cloth!

George pulled one out and removed its cover. It was a silver sugar bowl!

"Nancy!" Bess breathed. "You found Mrs. Campbell's heirlooms!"

"Not without your help," Nancy replied. "If—"

She stopped suddenly at a loud, creaking noise behind them. All three girls whirled around and saw the door being shut. A moment later, hollow laughter rang through the crypt. "Hahaha! You did not heed my warning. Now you will soon be dead, along with the Campbells and the smugglers I locked in the secret room those many years ago! Good-bye, Nancy Dreeeeeeeeeew!"

"T-that man d-didn't leave after all!" Bess whispered. "He's locked us in!"

George bit her lip. "We were so sure that he was gone that we left the key in the lock. That wasn't very smart."

"True," Nancy admitted. "We really goofed!"

"What'll we do now?" Bess asked worriedly.

Nancy played her light over the door. "We'll never be able to get it open," she said.

"That means we're trapped!" Tears began to well up in Bess's eyes.

"Don't worry, we'll find a way out," Nancy said firmly. But she sounded much more confident than she felt. "Let's check this place out inch by inch," she went on. "Maybe we'll find a loose slab of marble we can remove and squeeze through."

Desperately, the three detectives searched the walls, floor and ceiling, but the blocks were all firmly in place.

"Nothing," said George disconsolately. "It's solidly built. A mouse couldn't get out!"

She coughed. The air was becoming unbreathable.

Nancy inspected the coffin containing Mrs. Campbell's heirlooms.

"You know, the handles on each end are made out of three pieces. Two jut out of the wall, like brackets, and the third is a straight piece connecting the two. If we could remove one of the straight pieces, we could use it as a chisel to push the bolts out of the door hinges."

George nodded excitedly. "All we'd need is something to hammer it with."

"Right."

The girls looked around the floor. "Here, how about this?" Bess suggested and pointed to one of the supports of the coffin. It was made of metal.

"Great!" Nancy took the heavy cube and banged it against the coffin handle. The pin loosened and soon she held the rod-like piece in her hand. "Now for the hinge!"

She stepped up to the door. "George, would you hold this handle like a chisel, under the lower hinge. I'll hammer, and we'll see if we can get the bolt out. Bess, you shine the flashlight on the spot, okay?"

"Okay." Bess illuminated the hinge while Nancy and George went to work. At first the bolt did not budge, and once, Nancy's substitute hammer slipped, almost hitting George's hand.

"Nancy!" George cried out. "Don't do that!"

"Sorry," Nancy replied. "It was an accident. Here, let's try again."

Finally, after laboring for some time, she knocked the bolt out of the hinge far enough so that she could pull it out altogether.

"What a relief!" Bess gasped and set down the flashlight for a moment. "The air is becoming terrible in here. If we don't get out soon, we'll suffocate!"

"All we have to do now is take out the upper bolt," Nancy said.

Bess nodded. "I'll hold the chisel for you this time," she offered. "George, take the light."

It was hard to dislodge the rusty pin, and Nancy's wrist was aching as she hammered away. At last she managed to pull out the bolt, and the girls opened the door. With a cry of relief, they ran out of the dusty, dark crypt, and collapsed on the grass. Eagerly, they gulped in the cool night air.

"We'll have to report to the police," Nancy spoke up. "And we'd better take the heirlooms with us, in case the ghost decides to pay the cemetery another visit."

The girls carried the treasure to the car and drove to River Heights Police Headquarters. The sergeant on duty was surprised when they told him of their adventure. "We'll have to put that joker behind bars," he said angrily. "Do you have any idea who he could be?"

The girls shook their heads.

"Obviously it's someone who knew about the heirlooms," Nancy said. "It could have been one of the men who moved the Campbells years ago. Perhaps he heard about the treasure from Becker when visiting him in jail."

"Well, right now we'd better get back to Mrs. Campbell," George suggested. "I'm sure she's worried about us."

"Tell her the treasure is safe and sound," the sergeant said. "I'll have to keep it here as evidence. Perhaps she could drop by tomorrow to identify her property."

Mrs. Campbell was relieved when the girls arrived, and delighted that they had found her possessions. She offered them her guest room to spend the night.

Next morning, just as they were having breakfast, Mr. Hansen came over from next door. "Oh, hello, girls!" he cried out. "I'm glad to see you're back safe!"

"Safe?" Nancy asked, her eyebrows shooting up. "How did you know we were in danger?"

"Oh, well—" the man seemed at a loss for words. "You—were going to the cemetery yesterday. Didn't you say something about a ghost?"

Nancy nodded. "Yes, we did," she said.

"Well, did you find Mrs. Campbell's heirlooms?" the man continued.

"Yes," George spoke up. "We don't know yet if all her things were there. She'll have to go to the police station and identify them."

"Police station?" Mr. Hansen asked sharply. "You mean, you didn't bring the treasure back with you?"

"Of course not!" Bess told him. "We had to report what we found, and the police are keeping the heirlooms as evidence until they catch the thief!"

All the color seemed to have drained from Mr. Hansen's face. "Oh," he said. "Well, I think I'd better go back home. I have a few chores to do this morning."

"I think you'd better stay!" Nancy said. Suddenly, the pieces of the puzzle were falling together for her. She turned to George. "Quick, call the police," she whispered.

George looked puzzled, but did not question her friend. She went into the next room and made the call while Mr. Hansen stared at Nancy, not knowing what to make of the girl's request for him to stay.

"What do you need me for?" he finally asked.

"Some explanations," Nancy said. "Actually, I have all the explanations. All you have to do is confirm them.

"You knew about Mrs. Campbell's treasure, and you followed us to the cemetery last night. You thought Bess had the key to the crypt, so you waylaid her and threw her into an open grave. When you didn't find the key in her pocketbook, you shoved me in, too. Good thing you didn't succeed with George."

"I have no idea what you're talking about," the man said.

"Nancy, you're wrong!" Mrs. Campbell spoke up. "I've known Mr. Hansen for many years. He's always been a good friend!"

"He's only pretended to be," Nancy said. "He must have been hoping you'd show him that mysterious note so he could retrieve the treasure. When he found out you had called us, he tried to keep us away by throwing a rock with a threatening note into our car on the highway."

"Do you know what you're saying?" Mrs. Campbell was shocked.

"I do," Nancy replied confidently. "Twenty years ago Mr. Hansen plotted with Mr. Becker, the movers' foreman, to steal your heirlooms while you and your husband were moving to your new house. Becker stole your crypt key and had a duplicate made, then returned the key surreptitiously."

"This is ridiculous," Mr. Hansen cried out. "I refuse to listen to this nonsense any longer!" With that, he turned and headed for the door. When he opened it, he ran straight into the arms of two policemen!

"Lieutenant Green," one introduced himself. "And this is Sergeant Russo. I understand you have a problem?"

"We have evidence that this man is a thief!" Nancy said and pointed to Mr. Hansen. She told Lieutenant Green what had happened so far, then went on.

"My guess is that Mr. Hansen and Mr. Becker did not want to be seen together, so they used a secret code to communicate. Becker wrote Hansen a note saying where he had hidden the heirlooms, but dropped it in the attic by mistake. When the movers were ready to leave, he wanted to put the note into Hansen's mailbox, but couldn't find it. He wasn't able to write another one, because the rest of the men were waiting for him. The next day he was arrested for the robbery and went to jail."

"Why couldn't he have told Hansen about the hiding place while he was in jail?" Lieutenant Green asked.

"Hansen probably never visited him," Nancy said.

"He wanted no one to suspect he had any connections to a criminal. Also, even if Becker had told him, Hansen wouldn't have had the key!"

"What a story!" Mr. Hansen exclaimed. "It's all conjecture. There's no proof!"

Bess stared at him. "I bet you were the prowler yesterday. You wanted to find out what we knew, so you tried to eavesdrop on us."

"Of course," Nancy agreed.

"Then he followed us to the cemetery," George took up the story. "He played ghost to scare us, then kidnapped Bess to get the key."

"And when that didn't work, he locked us into the crypt," Nancy concluded.

"That just proves how silly your theory is," Mr. Hansen put in. "Mrs. Campbell knew you were at the cemetery. She would have sent the police if you hadn't returned. And I still wouldn't have the treasure."

"You went off to round up a couple of accomplices," Nancy said. "Then you came back to do away with us. Fortunately, we had escaped by then."

Mrs. Campbell stood up. "But Nancy, I still can't believe Mr. Hansen is a criminal. And you can't prove it!"

"Yes, I can," Nancy said. "How many people knew about that secret room in your basement that we discovered yesterday?"

"Why, no one," Mrs. Campbell replied. "I didn't even know until you told me about it."

"Mr. Hansen was here when we found it," Nancy went on. "And when he played ghost at the cemetery,

57

he said that we would soon be dead, just like those smugglers he locked into the secret room many years ago!"

Mr. Hansen's mouth dropped open when he realized that he had given himself away. He made a quick dash for the door, but Lieutenant Green and Sergeant Russo grabbed him before he could get out. Later, he confessed everything.

"I did work with Becker," he admitted. "I had arranged for a fence—someone to handle the loot for us. He was to meet Becker during Becker's drive from River Heights to the Campbells' new house. But something went wrong and he didn't make it. Becker didn't want to take the treasure home, because he was afraid the police might search his house if they ever traced the previous robbery to him. So he stashed the stuff in the woods. He knew he couldn't leave them there, so when he saw the crypt key at the Campbell's house, he had a duplicate made during his break."

"But why did he write you the note?" George asked.

"Just to let me know that things were under control. He probably figured once the fence was ready, we'd all go and retrieve the stuff."

"Only he couldn't deliver the note," Bess said. "Then he was arrested before he had another chance to contact you."

"That's right," Hansen said glumly.

"And now you'll join him in jail," Sergeant Russo added.

The police led the man away and the girls turned to comfort Mrs. Campbell, who was still shocked about the fact that she had lived next door to a criminal for ten years.

"Well, I'm glad he's behind bars," she said finally. "Nancy, I'm sorry I doubted you. You did a great job!"

"It was Bess who urged us to go to the cemetery, remember?" Nancy said.

Bess made a face. "I should have known better!" she declared. "Next time we'll send the police. That ghost scared me to death!"

"What ghost?" George asked, and they all broke out into gales of laughter.

THE *GEIST* OF MEYER'S MALL

"What a traffic jam!" Nancy Drew exclaimed, as she drove through a tangle of cars in front of the shopping mall.

"I've never seen so many people here," added George Fayne, who was sitting next to her. "I wonder if something's wrong?"

"Maybe they're having a big sale," Bess Marvin remarked from the back seat.

Nancy shook her head. "I doubt it. Business hasn't been good at Meyer's Mall for months. Not since the new shopping center opened downtown with the movie theater and the skating rink."

A policeman stood nearby, trying his best to unsnarl the tie-up. When the girls were able to inch close enough to him, Nancy stuck her head out of the window.

"What's going on, Officer?" she asked politely.

The man grinned. "Haven't you heard?" he replied. "Everyone's here to see the ghost!"

"Ghost!" all three girls remarked in unison.

63

The policeman nodded. "There are strange happenings in the mall these days," he said.

Just then, a break came in the traffic and Nancy pulled away, waving to the friendly policeman as she did.

"Hurrah!" Bess exclaimed. "We finally made it into the parking lot."

"What do you think this ghost business is all about?" dark-haired George asked.

Nancy shrugged. "Maybe we'll find out."

The girls parked the car and hurried into the mall.

"It looks as if they've painted and done repairs on the place," George commented when they walked through the glass door.

"There aren't any vacant stores anymore, either," Bess added. "The mall is suddenly thriving!"

Nancy and her friends moved through the crowd and headed toward the Chic Boutique, where they had been buying their clothes for a long time.

All at once, people were yelling and pointing at the ceiling.

A large blob was floating fifty feet overhead, swirling above the mall, its shape constantly changing, its color a greenish-yellow with an almost fluorescent glow.

A bank of escalators rose to an open, second-floor mezzanine, with a railing lined with planters full of gladiolas. The ghost swooped down and whimsically picked the flowers, raining them upon the onlookers.

The crowd roared with glee.

"This is the craziest thing I've ever seen!" Bess said through her laughter. "Look over there!"

A security guard had run up the escalator, yelling at

the ghost. The thing stopped pulling up plants and zoomed at the man. It knocked his hat off, to the delight of the crowd, then made his tie stand up straight in the air.

The guard turned and ran away, but the ghost stayed hot on his trail. It chased him down the escalator, pushing him into the small goldfish pond on the main floor.

The crowd laughed and applauded as the weird blob floated near them, constantly changing shape. Suddenly it turned bright red and rose quickly above people's heads, edging higher and higher to finally disappear into the ceiling.

The shoppers were talking excitedly as they dispersed, some of them heading out to the parking lot, but many staying to go into the stores.

"I'm beginning to understand why the mall is doing so well," Nancy said.

"Sure," George answered. "The ghost is attracting business!"

"Do you think it's a real ghost, Nancy?" Bess asked, her eyes still wide.

Nancy shook her head. "It looked real," she said, "but I've never heard of a haunted mall before!"

With the crowds breaking up, it was an easy walk to the dress shop. When the girls entered, old Mr. Lamell, the owner, and his granddaughter, Cassie, were busy waiting on customers.

The small, gray-haired man beamed when he saw the girls. "Guten tag!" he called in his native German. "Good day to my best customers!"

"Hi!" Cassie called from the cash register. The pretty

high school girl with dark hair and brown eyes was ringing up sale after sale, an event rarely seen in the Chic Boutique.

While the Lamells were busy, Nancy and her friends looked over the racks of clothes.

"What a selection!" George said, picking up a stylish pair of slacks. "Mr. Lamell always had good taste, but now his merchandise is just fabulous." She held the slacks in front of her and looked in a full-length mirror.

"Apparently business has gotten a lot better since the last time we were here," Nancy added.

"It's because of the *Geist*," came a voice from behind them.

They turned to see Mr. Lamell standing there, hands behind his back, a pixie smile on his face.

"*Geist?*" Bess repeated.

"That's German for ghost," Cassie said, as she joined them.

Mr. Lamell smiled, putting a hand to his forehead. "The words," he said. "Sometimes I get mixed up. How are my favorite customers?"

"We're doing great," Bess said.

"And, apparently, so are you," Nancy added.

"Can't complain," Mr. Lamell said. "Do you know that my Cassie is going to college this fall?"

"Grandfather . . . " Cassie said, blushing.

"But I'm proud of you." The old man put an arm around the girl, who was already a foot taller than he was.

"What's the story on the, er . . . *Geist*?" Nancy asked.

Mr. Lamell pursed his lips. "It began a couple of months ago," he said. "The local TV station was making a . . . what-do-you-call-it? . . . a commercial, for Central Bank over at the other end of the mall. All at once the Geist swooped down in front of them. They filmed it, and followed it into the shoe store, where it pulled box after box of shoes out of the cubbyholes."

"It was the funniest thing!" Cassie giggled. "Shoes flying all over the store!"

Mr. Lamell continued. "They showed their film on the news that night, and the Geist of Meyer's Mall has brought people here ever since. They come to see Hermie . . . "

"Hermie?" Nancy asked.

"That's Grandfather's nickname for the ghost," Cassie explained.

"Why Hermie?"

The little man suddenly looked nervous. "No special reason," he said. "It's just a name."

"Does the ghost come every night?" Bess inquired.

"No," Cassie answered. "It's very unpredictable. But the people don't seem to mind when it doesn't show. It appears often enough to make it worthwhile for them."

"Yes," Mr. Lamell added. "I haven't seen crowds like this since I was in show business."

"You were in show business?" Nancy asked.

"Back in the old country," the man answered. "That was a long time ago."

"What did you do?" George inquired, fascinated.

"Variety acts," Mr. Lamell returned. "You know, singing and dancing. I worked in the music halls . . . How do you call it over here?—Vaudeville."

Nancy noticed that Cassie had an odd look on her face. *Why had the atmosphere suddenly become tense?*

"So the ghost has helped business in the mall?" she said, changing the subject.

"Let me put it this way," Cassie said. "When you came in and bought that party dress a couple of months ago, I figured we'd be out of business before you'd be back again. Now, we're doing so well we're thinking about opening another store!"

"That's wonderful!" Bess exclaimed. "I'll be able to tell everyone that I knew you when you were poor and struggling."

Mr. Lamell excused himself and disappeared for a moment. When he returned, he was carrying three sundresses. He handed one to each of the girls.

"I remember your sizes," he said, then looked at Bess. "Unless Bessie's been eating candy bars again."

Bess beamed. "I'm the same size I was when I bought my last dress here."

"Take them, then," Mr. Lamell said, "with the compliments of the Chic Boutique. You have been such good patrons for years."

The girls protested, but the small man insisted, so they finally accepted the gifts. When they left the store a few minutes later, they passed the security guard who had been drenched in the goldfish pond. He was smiling and drying his hair with a towel.

"Strange," Nancy said, as the young detectives walked out of the mall. "That ghost business really has me wondering."

"It's the first time I've ever seen a ghost with a sense of humor," George added.

"Did you see how strangely Mr. Lamell reacted when he talked about Hermie and his own past?" Nancy said. "By the way, someone's been following us ever since we went into the boutique."

Bess and George turned around. Twenty feet behind them, a scruffy-looking man was staring at them through the glass doors of the mall. When he saw them looking at him, he ducked quickly into the building.

"There's more to this than meets the eye," Nancy declared.

Later that night, she sat in her room reading up on ghosts and hauntings. Although most reports of ghostly behavior were frightening, there were cases where people had reported mischievous spirits, usually called poltergeists, or noisy ghosts. It came from the German root word, Geist.

"Nancy!" Hannah Gruen, the Drews' housekeeper, called out. "We have fresh strawberries down here!"

"Coming!" Nancy answered, putting the book down.

When she got to the kitchen, her father, Carson Drew, was already eating strawberries and whipped cream.

Hannah stood with her hands on her hips, shaking her head. "That's the fastest I've seen you move since you thought the house was on fire."

"Very funny," Nancy said, quickly digging into the sweet delight.

"Dad," she asked, "aren't ghosts supposed to be the spirits of people who died in a particular place?"

Her father smiled. "Well, I'm a better lawyer than a

ghost chaser," he joked, "but that has always been my understanding."

"Was there ever a house where Meyer's Mall now stands?"

"No," Mr. Drew answered.

"Are you sure?"

"I am. When I was a boy, that property was a pasture for sheep. Then a little carnival was put up. You know, pony rides and snow cone stands. It wasn't much by today's standards, but I spent many happy hours out there. It made me sad when they finally built the mall."

"Then how do we explain the ghost?" Nancy asked.

"Maybe it's the spirit of a disgruntled sheep!" Hannah laughed.

"Maybe," Nancy said, her mind drifting.

When she was finished eating, she excused herself and went to the phone to call Cassie Lamell.

"Hello?" the girl answered after the second ring.

"Cassie, this is Nancy Drew. Is your grandfather home?"

"No, he isn't," Cassie returned.

"Good," Nancy said. "I wanted to talk to you alone. Mind if I drop by?"

"Of course not," Cassie exclaimed. "Grandfather will be at the store until late doing inventory, and I'd love the company."

Within ten minutes, Nancy was sitting next to Cassie on the Lamells' living room sofa.

"Congratulations on being accepted into college," she said.

71

"Thanks," Cassie replied, lowering her dark eyes. "I suppose I owe that to the ghost. Things had been so bad that Grandfather was afraid he couldn't afford to send me. But since Hermie appeared on the scene, things have been different."

"Your folks passed away sometime ago, didn't they?" Nancy asked.

The girl nodded. "They died when I was very young. I don't even remember them."

"I noticed a strange look on your face when I was talking to your grandfather about his show business career," Nancy said.

Cassie grimaced slightly. "I didn't realize it was that obvious," she said. "It's just that he has never talked to me about his past very much. I knew he had been in show business, but he never mentioned exactly what he did. I've heard him singing, though, and he's got a terrible voice!"

Both girls laughed.

"Does he keep any memorabilia around concerning the old days?" Nancy inquired.

"He has a couple of trunks in the attic that might have something in them," Cassie replied. "But he's never opened them for me. Would you like to go look?"

"Your grandfather wouldn't mind?"

"Well, he's never told me *not* to look in them."

Excited, the girls went up the attic stairs and pushed open the overhead door.

"Funny," Nancy said as she climbed into the stuffy room, "the light is on. Have you or your grandfather been up here lately?"

"I haven't," Cassie replied. "And I don't think he can climb the stairs any more."

"Well, someone's been up here recently and forgotten to turn off the light!"

"Nancy!" Cassie exclaimed, pointing to a corner of the room. "The trunks are gone!"

The girls examined the spot where the trunks had been. There were two clear rectangles on the dusty floor, and drag marks all the way to the door.

Nancy's mind was racing. "When we left the store tonight," she said, "the security guard who tangled with the ghost was just coming in. Do you know him?"

"He's a distant cousin of mine from the old country," Cassie said. "His name's Gunther Martin. When he came to America, Grandfather got him a job at the mall."

"How long ago was that?"

Cassie put a finger to her lips. "Four or five months ago, I think."

Just then, Nancy saw something on the floor, yellowed with age. "What's this?" she asked, picking it up.

"It looks like an old theater program," Cassie commented. "Maybe it fell out of one of the trunks!"

She opened up the slim, stiff paper book. It was filled with what appeared to be German writing, and in the middle of the first page was the fading photograph of a young man with intense eyes. His arms were folded across his chest and he wore a turban on his head.

"That's Grandfather!" Cassie exclaimed.

"It sure looks like him," Nancy agreed. "But what does the caption under the picture mean?" She read, *"Lamell der Grosse, und sein tanzender Geist."*

Cassie shrugged. "I'm sorry, but I don't know German."

Nancy stared at the picture. "Mind if I take this with me for tonight?"

Cassie shook her head. "Not at all. I'm getting intrigued myself."

It was late by the time Nancy returned home. She went right to bed, dreaming about strawberries and ghosts.

When she woke up the next morning, her father had already gone to work. Hannah was out in the yard, beating the dust out of a throw rug with a cane.

"Good morning, Hannah," Nancy called.

"You mean, good afternoon," Hannah retorted. "You've slept the morning away!"

Nancy walked up to the housekeeper, who was like a mother to her. "Don't you have relatives in Germany?" she asked.

"Some," Hannah replied.

"I don't suppose you know any German."

"No, but my niece, Effie Schneider, does. Why?"

"I have something that needs translating," Nancy said.

"I'll call Effie," Hannah offered.

While waiting for Hannah, Nancy showered and put on the sundress that Mr. Lamell had given her. Then she spoke to Effie on the telephone. Thirty minutes later, she walked into the Chic Boutique with the program in hand.

Mr. Lamell looked apprehensive when he saw her. "I had a feeling I'd see you today, after Cassie told me you were over last night," he said. "She's not here. It's her day off."

74

Nancy nodded. Then she opened the program and put it on the top of the counter. *"Lamell Der Grosse und sein tanzender Geist,"* she read. "Lamell the Great, and his dancing ghost."

Mr. Lamell smiled sadly.

"You were a magician in Europe, specializing in large visual illusions," the girl detective went on.

The man nodded. "A very famous magician," he added.

"You hadn't practiced your trade since coming to this country," Nancy continued, "but you kept all the magician tools in your attic. Your business wasn't doing well and you worried about how you could afford to send Cassie to college. Then along came Gunther Martin, who, unless I miss my guess, was also in show business. Another magician?"

Mr. Lamell ran a hand through his short gray hair. "He was an acrobat in the circus."

"Perfect," Nancy said. "So, you got him the job here, and the two of you revived your famous 'dancing ghost' to advertise Meyer's Mall. You brought your trunks over here, and sometimes you stay late for 'inventory', so you can rig up your visual gags."

"It's quite an art form," Mr. Lamell said. "A great deal of it is done with special invisible wires, popularized by Blackstone the Magician many years ago."

"And it worked," Nancy said.

"Until now," the man returned.

Nancy put her hand on his shoulder. "I'm not trying to cause you any trouble," she said. "You didn't hurt anyone. You don't charge anything for your 'shows,' and all the merchants who've been working with you on this are happy. The night I was here, everyone loved it. I think you should stop, though. You're perpetrating a minor fraud."

"You're right," Mr. Lamell said. "I've been feeling guilty about it myself."

Nancy left soon after that. Something bothered her, and she turned around quickly. The man who had been following her and the girls the night before was back again. He stood near the door of the boutique, watching her go out of the mall. However, he did not trail her.

That afternoon, the telephone rang at the Drew home. Nancy answered to Mr. Lamell on the other end, his voice cracking as he spoke. "Nancy, something terrible has happened!"

"What?"

"I don't have time to talk. Meet me by the trash dumpster behind the mall. If I'm not there, wait for me. Please come. I have no one else to turn to."

"I'll be right there," Nancy promised, and hung up.

Quickly, she drove to the mall. When she arrived, the area around the dumpster was deserted.

Not knowing the reason for Mr. Lamell's secrecy, she pulled her car up behind the dumpster so that it would be difficult to spot from the shopping center, and waited.

A few minutes later, Mr. Lamell appeared at the back door of his boutique, carrying a large trash bag. He looked nervously around, then walked up to the dumpster and deposited the bag.

The young detective got out of her car and approached him.

"Oh, Nancy," he whispered, "I'm so frightened, I can hardly think."

"What's happened?" she asked.

"After you left today, a man came to me in the store. He had overheard our conversation."

"I think I saw him when I was leaving," Nancy said.

"He's a crook," Mr. Lamell went on. "He and his cohorts have been . . . how do you say . . . working the crowds, picking pockets. Now that he knows who makes the ghost happen, he wants me to rig up a special show for tonight, one that draws a lot of people, while he's robbing the Central Bank!"

"I'll call the police," Nancy offered. "We'll catch the whole gang!"

"No!" Mr. Lamell said, horrified. "You can't. They've kidnapped Cassie!"

"What!"

"If I don't do what they say, they'll hurt her!" The man was shaking with fear. "If anything happens to that girl, I don't know what I'll do. I'm afraid to bring the police in, Nancy. Please, we have to handle this on our own!"

"All right," Nancy agreed. "What exactly did they tell you?"

"They want me to make a big *Geist* display, at eight o'clock, with lots of noise," Mr. Lamell explained. "Since it's Friday, the bank will be open late."

"What about Cassie?" Nancy asked.

"They plan to bring her here and hold her on the

mezzanine, where you saw the ghost pick the flowers yesterday. If everything goes well, they'll set her free."

"Hmmm," Nancy said, a finger to her lips. "I have an idea, but I'll need some help. Let me call Bess and George. I also need to get hold of Gunther Martin, your assistant."

Mr. Lamell nodded, taking Nancy's hand. "Thank you," he said, his voice catching in his throat. "I don't know what I'd do without you."

"Thank me later," Nancy returned. "When this is all over."

That evening, the young detective stood in a darkened office that overlooked the mall area from the second floor. The glass had been removed from the window to let a mass of fine guide wires through. They converged at a panel in the office from where the *Geist* of Meyer's Mall was controlled during his frequent flights through the building.

"Nancy," came George's voice over the walkie-talkie. "Can you hear me?"

Nancy pushed a button on her receiver.

"Yes," she said. "What's up?"

"I'm positioned in the bank," George answered through the static. "No one can see me from the lobby. So far everything's quiet."

"Okay," Nancy said. "Keep me posted. Bess? Are you there?"

"Bess Marvin reporting in," came Bess's official-sounding voice. "Everything's normal here at the toy store."

"Wait for my signal," Nancy said. "Over and out."

Mr. Lamell came into the dark office. "We are ready!"

Nancy nodded and looked out the window. Just below her on the mezzanine, several crates had been set up, almost blocking the view of the mall. Only one good spot was left.

"Well, we're . . . " she began, but was cut off by the crackle of the radio.

"Nancy!" George whispered anxiously. "Come in!"

Nancy was about to answer when she saw two people on the mezzanine. One was Cassie! A man was holding her by the arms—the same man who had been following Nancy!

The girl detective motioned for Mr. Lamell to look out the window, then pushed the button on the two-way radio. "This is Nancy," she answered. "Over."

"Ohhh," George said in a crackly voice. "They're here. They're checking their watches!"

"Okay, stand by!"

The pretty detective looked at Mr. Lamell. "Time to put Operation Poltergeist into effect!"

The man nodded. "Keep the fingers crossed!"

He moved to the control panel. "Got a full house out there tonight," he said, as he pushed the lever that started the mechanical howling.

A loud, eerie moan filled the mall. Then, the magician began manipulating the wires. Precision, Mr. Lamell had told Nancy, was of utmost importance in the dancing ghost business, and he had worked on this particular trick all day long.

There was a crash, and four weird forms came

through the skylight. They were really thick plastic bags with small motors inside that propelled them around and changed their shapes while a series of lights kept alternating the internal colors.

"I'm getting into position," Nancy said, and hurried out of the office.

On the first floor, Bess watched as the ghosts swept above the heads of the people, who were shrieking with pleasure. Then the poltergeists dipped down even more, scattering the crowds in confusion.

George watched from the well of an empty desk in the bank, as the robbers pulled guns and took money from the teller cages. No customers were entering the bank; everyone was busy enjoying the ghosts.

"They've got the money," George whispered into her radio. "They'll be coming out any second!"

Bess picked up the message in the toy store. She turned to the three salespeople next to her. "Get ready," she said, then picked up a bucketful of marbles. So did the others.

The four dancing ghosts dangled from Mr. Lamell's invisible wires and started spinning a circle in front of the bank, chasing all the watchers away. This maneuver left a large opening.

When the thieves charged out of the bank, they found themselves not covered by the crowd as they had expected, but conspicuously visible in the clear spot. Frantically, they tried to hurry away.

"Now!" Bess commanded from her position near the front of the toy store. She and the salespeople threw bucketsful of marbles onto the floor, right in front of the criminals!

The *Geist* of Meyer's Mall

The crooks ran, but with the tiny spheres underfoot, they were soon skidding all over, finally crashing to the floor as a whole contingent of security people moved in to subdue them. The crowd laughed and applauded, thinking it was all part of the show.

The man who was holding Cassie on the mezzanine angrily dragged her away. Mr. Lamell saw it and pulled another wire. "Come on, Hermie," he said. "Don't let me down!"

Hermie swooped from the ceiling. Gracefully but quickly, he moved toward Cassie and her abductor.

The man heard the noise, and turned just in time to see the *Geist* coming at him!

It hit him hard, thanks to the brick Nancy had loaded inside, and knocked him out of the way long enough for the young detective to dash out of her hiding place and grab Cassie by the hand.

The man yelled and chased the girls, who were running along the mezzanine. All of a sudden Gunther Martin swung out of the rafters on a long rope. He arced down toward the kidnapper and grabbed him by the collar.

The momentum carried both of them up and over the mezzanine rail, where Gunther let the man plummet, arms flailing, into the same fish pond that the security guard had landed in the night before.

The crowd roared. Nancy began to understand that the people had never really believed in the ghost. They had just come to enjoy the show rigged up by a master magician!

The dripping kidnapper climbed out of the pond and walked into the arms of waiting security, while sirens could be heard approaching in the distance.

Cassie and Nancy went to the edge of the rail and looked down. "Are you okay?" the young detective asked her friend.

The girl nodded and gave Nancy a hug. Just then, Mr. Lamell joined them.

"I'm glad this is all over," he said. "But you know, I'm going to miss old Hermie! He doesn't want to go back in the trunk."

Nancy smiled, then waved her arms. "Ladies and gentlemen," she called, and the crowd quieted down, looking expectantly at her. "I'd like you to meet the man responsible for all these wonderful effects. Here is Lamell the Great, and his dancing ghost, Hermie!"

The shoppers cheered loudly and Mr. Lamell bowed, tears in his eyes. He was happy to hear the applause of an audience again!

"You know," Nancy whispered, "why don't you clear your act with the authorities? I can't see anyone objecting, and the shoppers would just love to see Hermie every once in a while."

Mr. Lamell's eyes twinkled. "Not only Hermie," he said. "Meyer's Mall can have a different ghost every week!"

WITCHES'
BREW

Nancy Drew was humming happily when she stepped into the elevator. The young detective was glad to be in New York again and looking forward to a visit with her Aunt Eloise.

A mysterious note from Eloise Drew had prompted the trip. "Come at once, if possible," her aunt had written. "Something strange is going on around here."

The elevator shot up and Nancy wondered about the message. What could it mean? A moment later, as she stepped into the corridor, a woman charged straight at her, almost knocking her down! Nancy staggered back and barely managed to keep her balance. The woman, who was small, slender, and middle-aged, was obviously distraught. Without apologizing, she rushed into the old-fashioned elevator, slammed the door shut, and pressed the "down" button.

"She sure was in a hurry, wasn't she?" said another woman, who had just stepped out of an apartment two

85

doors down from Aunt Eloise. She was tall and elegantly dressed, and her jet black hair fell down to her shoulders. "Are you all right?" she inquired.

"Yes, I am, thank you," Nancy replied with a smile. Then she walked to her aunt's door and pressed the bell.

"Nancy, my dear, come in!" Eloise Drew gave her niece a big hug and drew her into the comfortable living room. "Did you have a good trip?"

"I did," Nancy said. "I got here safe and sound, but a woman almost ran me down by the elevator."

"Oh?" Miss Drew's eyebrows shot up. "What did she look like?"

"Small, blond, about your age. Seemed upset."

"Oh, I bet that was Dottie Hughes. She used to be a good friend of mine until—well, it all has to do with why I asked you to come here."

"Tell me about it!" Nancy urged.

"Something strange is going on next door to me," Aunt Eloise began. "It started about six months ago. I hear eerie chanting from Apartment 307 now and then, and once in a while someone wails and screams. I think a bunch of witches meet in that place!"

Nancy laughed. "Aunt Eloise, be serious!"

"I am!" insisted her handsome aunt, who was a schoolteacher. "You'll find—"

Just then she was interrupted by a loud screech, that turned into a drawn-out wail.

"What was that?" Nancy asked, taken aback.

"Maybe one of the evil spirits that seem to have invaded our building," Aunt Eloise replied with a weak grin.

"You're half serious, aren't you?" Nancy stared at her aunt, then stood up and went to the window. The wail had turned into an angry growl, and Nancy looked toward its direction. She was just in time to see a huge, black cat leap onto the balcony of the next apartment.

Nancy broke into a peal of laughter as the cat sat down and began to wash its face. "Come and look," she said to her aunt. "There's your evil spirit, licking itself."

Aunt Eloise joined Nancy at the window and chuckled. "I suppose I'm getting edgy," she admitted. "But really, Nancy, you should hear those eerie voices. Dottie Hughes, who also lives on this floor, used to visit me all the time. But since she started attending those meetings at Madame Arnette's, she's avoided me and all her other friends. And she acts strange, as if she doesn't know what she's doing."

"I could see *that* in the hallway," Nancy said thoughtfully. "And another woman confirmed it. She saw it, too."

"You met another one of my neighbors?"

Nancy nodded. "Very tall, chic, with black hair—"

"Mrs. Egmont," Aunt Eloise broke in. "She's an actress. She's a very nice person, although she tends to be a bit melodramatic at times. She lives on the other side of Madame Arnette, and we've been talking about the strange goings-on. She hears the noises too, and believe me, Nancy, she's also convinced that Madame Arnette is a witch!"

"Don't you think you're jumping to conclusions?" Nancy asked.

"I have something that'll prove my suspicion is

right," Eloise Drew said. She stood up and went to her desk, where she picked up a small object.

"I found this lying in the hall," she told Nancy, handing her an oblong, metal pendant.

Nancy examined it closely. "It's Diana!" she exclaimed. "Diana the huntress or goddess of the moon."

"A witches' charm," Aunt Eloise added. "Worship of Diana was part of witch ceremonies in Europe. The covens used to convene by the light of the full moon."

"You have a point there," Nancy agreed. "What do you think we should do?"

"If you could infiltrate the coven and see what these people are up to—"

Nancy's eyes sparkled as she interrupted her aunt excitedly, "Good idea! I'll become a witch! That's a cover I've never used before. It should be very interesting."

Aunt Eloise held up a hand. "Shh! Did you hear that?"

Nancy fell quiet and nodded. The sound of stealthy footsteps in the corridor came nearer and halted outside the apartment!

Nancy stood up silently and tiptoed to the door. She twisted the knob cautiously to one side, then jerked the door inward.

A small, blond woman almost fell into the room!

"Why, Mrs. Hughes!" Nancy said.

The woman looked flustered. "Oh," she stammered, "I—I wanted to talk to Eloise—"

"Yes, Dottie," Aunt Eloise came up behind Nancy, "what can I do for you?"

88

"I—I wondered if you found an oblong pendant," Mrs. Hughes went on. "I think I dropped it in the hallway. It means a lot to me."

"Why, yes, I did find it," Eloise Drew replied. "My niece Nancy and I were just looking at it."

Mrs. Hughes nodded absently at the girl, who smiled. "It's a very interesting piece," Nancy said, and handed the ornament to the woman. "Wearing it gives you the protection of Diana, doesn't it?"

Mrs. Hughes stared at her openmouthed.

"I know all about Diana," Nancy confided in a conspiratorial tone. "I used to belong to a coven in my home town."

"Then you believe in the power of the occult?" Mrs. Hughes asked, obviously impressed.

"I certainly do," Nancy replied.

"The power of Diana has been of great help to me," Mrs. Hughes went on. "In fact, through the goddess, I have been able to contact my dead husband. I can't tell you how happy that has made me!"

Nancy's eyes clouded. "A dear friend of mine died last year. I'd love to be able to communicate with her . . ." Her voice trailed off.

"I could bring you to our next meeting, if you'd like," Mrs. Hughes suggested. "It's tomorrow, on the night of the full moon. I'll introduce you to our leader, Madame Arnette. She may be able to intercede with the goddess for you."

"Could you?" Nancy asked excitedly. "I would really be grateful."

Mrs. Hughes promised to pick her up at nine the

following evening, then, clutching her pendant, said good-bye and left.

"What did I tell you?" Aunt Eloise said. "Madame Arnette is a witch. And you were wonderful, Nancy! Your act was just great!"

Nancy shrugged. "I hate to lie, but this poor woman has obviously been duped. If I can help her, and others in that group, it'll be worth my fib about being a witch."

Nancy and Mrs. Hughes arrived promptly at Madame Arnette's the next evening. The young detective's heart skipped a beat at what she saw inside.

Heavy curtains, closely drawn, hung across a row of windows. In the middle of the room stood a black table shaped like a coffin. Around it, a circle about nine feet wide was drawn in white chalk on the bare wooden floor. Dim light came from concealed lamps, throwing shadows across the room. The scent of incense was almost overpowering.

Nancy shivered. The wall opposite the windows was covered with drawings of wild goats and leering horned devils. On another wall hung a flat sculpture of a sphinx with its mouth open.

A huge statue of the goddess Diana, holding her bow and arrow, dominated the room. It stood against the curtains in an atmosphere heavy with menace.

Nancy bit her lips. What, she wondered, had she gotten herself into? One detail of the spooky scene nagged at her mind. She could not recall ever having seen a sphinx with an open mouth.

Witches' Brew

The mistress of this uncanny establishment, Nancy decided, certainly looked like a witch. Madame Arnette had a long face with a sharp nose and yellow teeth. Her nails were like talons, painted blood red. Her rusty hair stood in a frizzy halo around her head. She wore a long, black robe with batwing sleeves and earrings with strings of ebony beads.

When Mrs. Hughes introduced Nancy, Madame Arnette gave the young detective a penetrating stare from her glittering black eyes.

"So, you would pierce the mysteries of the dead!" she muttered. "Beware! They may not wish you well!"

Nevertheless, she asked Nancy for the name of her friend and where the deceased had been buried.

"Her name is Linda Brown, and her grave is at Saint Barbara's Churchyard on the West Side," Nancy replied, thinking fast. She had heard her aunt mention Saint Barbara's once.

"Very well," droned the high priestess. "Two days from now we will try to summon your friend. The powers of Diana are strongest during the full moon."

The night's ceremony began. The witches of the coven, who had been assembling, looked excited, almost hysterical. They grouped themselves around the table, inside the white chalk circle. Nancy and Mrs. Hughes joined them. All clasped hands. Madame Arnette switched off the lights and pulled the heavy curtain drawstring.

Moonlight flooded the room with silver, leaving the statue of Diana etched dramatically in black, eerie and beautiful.

Witches' Brew

Madame Arnette began to sing in a hoarse voice:
 Abracadabra, all is well,
 As long as we know Diana's spell.
The other women took up the weird chant and repeated it. Then the high priestess left and returned a moment later with a large cauldron, which she placed carefully on the table.

"This is witches' brew," she intoned. "We must all drink to the goddess Diana."

The scene made Nancy think of the witches in Shakespeare's *Macbeth*, which she had studied in high school English class. She could not help repeating under her breath the witches' weird lines:
 "Double, double, toil and trouble!
 Fire burn and cauldron bubble!"
Madame Arnette was ladling the brew from the cauldron into black goblets, offering one to each woman. Nancy watched as the others drank eagerly. Madame Arnette, however, barely touched her goblet to her lips, and set it down without drinking.

This is where I join her, Nancy thought, looking for a place to spill her brew. She spotted a snake plant growing by the window, and eased her way over to it surreptitiously, making sure the high priestess did not notice her.

"I'm sure you'll enjoy this more than I would!" she told the plant in an undertone, pouring the liquid into the loam. "To your good health—or abracadabra—or whatever witches say!"

When Nancy went back to the table, she noticed that the witches were behaving strangely. They seemed to sway in unison. Their eyes were glazed, and they looked dully at their leader. Mrs. Hughes was in the same condition as the rest.

Thank goodness I didn't drink anything, thought Nancy. *The stuff in that cauldron must be a witches' brew of some kind!*

Everyone sat down at the table. Madame Arnette announced that she was about to summon the goddess.

A weird greenish light suddenly emanated from the open mouth of the sphinx behind her. The beam combined with the moonlight to bathe the head witch in a ghostly aura as she intoned her chant.

Nancy felt a prickling at the back of her neck. *Wow!* she thought. *Madame Arnette certainly has a flair for drama!*

"I conjure you, O great Diana, to hear our supplications!" the witch cried out. "Goddess of the moon! One of our members would speak through you tonight, to her dear one who departed this life three years ago!"

Suddenly, from the mouth of the sphinx, came a voice, low and clear. The coven gasped. Diana was in their midst!

"One of those assembled here comes from the state of Wyoming!" the goddess intoned.

"I am from Wyoming!" cried Mrs. Hughes.

"Your husband would have you know that he is well in the land beyond the grave," said the spectral voice. "He asks if you remember the lilacs in your garden long ago in Wyoming."

Mrs. Hughes looked transformed with joy. "Oh, yes, John, I do!" she exclaimed.

94

Diana murmured, "His voice is fading. But he will come to you again. I can say no more now."

Diana fell silent, then spoke again. "I hear from someone named—Maria," she said slowly. "Maria wants to tell Joey to keep on trying. He will succeed if he is persevering!"

"Maria is my sister!" one of the women exclaimed. "She's talking to my nephew Joey, who is having great difficulty in school. I'm so happy she said he'll succeed!"

The next silence was longer, then Diana continued in a hesitant tone. "The husband of the woman from Wyoming is coming back. He wants to warn her that he sees danger, grave danger!"

Mrs. Hughes was aghast. "Ask him what he means!" she begged. "Please, don't let him go!"

"He tells you not to venture abroad. That is all he will say. Now he has gone."

After that, the goddess fell silent. However, the meeting was far from over. Nancy watched with fascination as Madame Arnette began to sway and shake.

"The future," she murmured. "We will now see the future."

"My brother," one woman asked. "Will he live? He is so ill. He's been in the hospital for weeks."

"You must pray for him," the witch intoned. "Pray!"

She told one of her followers to look for another job, a second to beware of a man named Peter, and a third to expect a new romance in her life. It went on in that manner for several minutes, then she came out of her trance and the seance was over. Madame Arnette informed the coven that the next meeting would take place two nights later. As the women filed out of the apartment, Nancy noticed that each dropped money into an urn held by the high priestess.

The young detective produced a bill from her pocketbook, but, using a sleight of hand, palmed it skillfully up her sleeve instead of depositing it in the container.

Then she saw Madame Arnette beckoning Mrs. Hughes to stay behind. That gave her an idea. She rushed back to her aunt's apartment, dashed through the living room, and opened the door to the balcony. A stone ledge connected all the balconies on that side of the building, and Nancy quickly climbed over the banister and stepped onto it. Carefully, she moved along the open space high above the sidewalk. With her back to the wall, and holding her breath, she reached Madame Arnette's balcony and climbed over the balustrade.

A moment later she was peering into the witch's living room. Inside, she could see Madame Arnette talking earnestly to Mrs. Hughes.

If only I could hear what they're saying! Nancy thought. She found the window slightly ajar and raised it cautiously. The voices inside became audible.

"Your husband is most anxious to keep communicating with you," she heard Madame Arnette tell the excited Mrs. Hughes. "But Diana expects you to be suitably grateful. She looks favorably on large offerings at her shrine."

"Anything!" cried Mrs. Hughes. "I will pay anything!"

She emptied her purse on the table, then said good-bye. After she had left, Madame Arnette picked up the money and went through the door to the adjoining room. Moving to the next window, the girl detective was able to see the witch leader was in a luxuriously decorated bedroom.

Madame Arnette took a green loose-leaf notebook from the top drawer of her bureau, and in it she wrote a few lines. She replaced the notebook with a smile, then strolled over to the window.

A chill went down Nancy's spine. *If that woman looks out, I've had it!* the girl detective thought and quickly retreated. She climbed over the balcony onto the stone ledge and stood flat against the wall, hardly daring to breathe, her eyes fixed on Madame Arnette's bedroom window. A few moments passed, but nothing happened.

Cautiously, Nancy went back to Eloise Drew's apartment and stepped into the living room. At the same moment, her aunt came in with a bedtime snack. Nancy collapsed into an easy chair and related her experience.

When she had finished, she had calmed down enough to enjoy a piece of homemade devil's food cake. "Hm," she said. "This is as sinfully good as its namesake, the devil, is sinfully bad. And, talking about the devil, I intend to keep an eye on Madame Arnette. She's up to no good."

Next morning, Nancy was in the kitchen finishing the breakfast dishes, when she heard the door of a neighboring apartment shut with a bang. She dropped the dishtowel and ran to peek out the door in time to see Madame Arnette heading toward the elevator. Nancy hastily told her aunt that she was going to tail their neighbor. She slipped into the corridor and heard the elevator creaking its way to the ground floor.

Better take the stairs, Nancy advised herself. *If I wait for the elevator, she'll be gone.*

The young detective raced down and reached the door of the building in time to see Madame Arnette disappear around the corner. Quickly Nancy dodged through the crowd after her, hiding in a doorway when the witch looked back suspiciously. Madame Arnette did not see her, and Nancy resumed her surveillance when the woman went on.

After several blocks, Madame Arnette entered a small, grimy-looking office. Stenciled on the window in gilt letters was the legend *Ponsonby Investigations.*

A bus stop in front of the window provided cover for Nancy, who mingled with the crowd waiting for the next bus. Unobtrusively, she looked through the window. She was in time to see Madame Arnette greet a large man with a beard. The witch handed him a sheet from a loose-leaf notebook. He nodded, put it in his pocket, then went to his desk and picked up several papers, which he gave to the witch. At that point, Madame Arnette wrote out a check for him, then took the documents and turned to leave.

Quickly, Nancy ducked around the corner of the building. She watched the woman step out and go back in the direction from where she had come.

A moment later, the bearded man who Nancy assumed was Mr. Ponsonby, himself, emerged from the office. He locked the door behind him, then briskly walked to a yellow Ford that was parked across the street.

I'd better follow him, Nancy thought, and looked around for a taxi. Luckily, one stopped for her just as the investigator eased his car into the traffic.

"Could you please follow that Ford?" Nancy asked the driver and handed him a bill. "Don't let him get away!"

The man grinned. "I'll do my best, miss," he said. "Not many drivers in this city can get ahead of me."

Ponsonby went across Central Park to the West Side and stopped on one of the side streets.

"That's interesting," thought Nancy. *"He's going into a church!"*

She looked above the door for the name. It was Saint Barbara's! Now she understood why Ponsonby was there.

After paying her driver, Nancy followed the detective inside. She was in time to see Ponsonby disappearing into the registry.

"He's gone to check the records!" she muttered. "He won't find any Linda Brown listed there."

Nancy was standing near the altar, beside a statue of the church's patron saint, Saint Barbara, when Ponsonby came out again. He looked puzzled.

He'd better not see me, she thought, and ducked behind the statue of Saint Barbara.

But her hasty movement dislodged a candle, which clattered to the floor.

Ponsonby turned instantly.

Nancy froze for a moment, realizing she was trapped. Then she saw a door in the corner leading to the belltower. She dived toward it, hoping her pursuer wouldn't see her, and raced up the winding stone stairway. Her heart was pounding, her breath coming faster and faster. Finally she stumbled through the door leading to the platform around the church bell at the top of the tower. She tripped, and grabbed at the dangling bell rope to save her fall.

As the noise of the bell reverberated through the building, Nancy heard heavy footsteps on the stairs.

Hastily, she sneaked behind the open door and waited. Ponsonby rushed through the door, across the belltower, and looked over the parapet.

Nancy slipped around the door, slammed it shut, and turned the key in the lock. Then she hurried downstairs and out of the church. She ran two blocks and caught the crosstown bus back to her aunt's apartment. Madame Arnette, still holding the papers Ponsonby had given her, was waiting for the elevator when Nancy arrived, but the young sleuth made sure she wasn't seen. Apparently the witch had stopped off somewhere on the way home.

What's she going to do with those documents? Nancy wondered. *I think another sortie over to her place is in order.*

Five minutes later, the persistent girl detective edged herself along the ledge between the balconies and was rewarded with a glimpse of Madame Arnette in her bedroom, inserting the sheets from the detective agency into her green loose-leaf notebook, which she then placed in the top drawer of the bureau.

I bet it's information on dead people—relatives of Madame Arnette's clients, Nancy thought. *If only I could prove it!*

"Are you through with sleuthing for today?" her aunt asked over lunch. "Bloomingdale's is having a sale. I thought we could do some shopping."

"Good idea," Nancy said. "I don't think watching Madame Arnette is going to be any more productive at this point. I have an idea what her racket is. All I have to figure out is how to get the evidence."

The young detective and her aunt spent a delightful, if exhausting, afternoon trying on slacks, dresses, and shoes. Then, as a special treat, they had dinner at the Russian Tea Room, Nancy's favorite New York restaurant.

The phone rang as they were getting ready for bed. It was Ned Nickerson, Nancy's boyfriend. He was in town for a football conference and was staying at a hotel only two blocks away.

"I'll be free by tomorrow evening," he told Nancy, "and then we can have some fun."

Next day, while Aunt Eloise was teaching school, Nancy spent the afternoon at the Museum of Natural History.

When she returned to her aunt's apartment, she found Madame Arnette on the doorstep, all smiles.

"Miss Drew," the woman purred. "I have interceded with Diana on your behalf and she is willing to reach your friend, Linda Brown. But she feels the aura would be strongest in the vicinity of the burial place. Would you be free to accompany me there this evening?"

Nancy's mind was racing. She knew this must be a trap. But if she refused to go, she might never be able to prove Madame Arnette's dishonesty.

"Yes, of course," she told the witch. "What time would you like to start out?"

"My car is in the garage around the corner," explained Madame Arnette. "We can leave at once."

Nancy quickly decided to call her friend Ned for help.

"I'll just get my purse," she told Madame Arnette and ducked into the bedroom. Hastily, she dialed Ned's hotel, holding her breath till he answered.

"Thank goodness you're there," she said in relief, and quickly told him what was happening.

"It will take me about five minutes to go downstairs, hop into my car, and drive over to your aunt's apartment," Ned said. "Just stall your witch long enough for me to get there." He hung up.

Nancy went back into the living room. Aunt Eloise and Madame Arnette were talking about a Broadway play. The girl detective had read the review, and quickly launched into a lengthy description of the critic's point of view. She went on and on, until Madame Arnette became impatient. "Well, we'd better go," the woman declared. "Diana does not like to be kept waiting."

With a pretty smile, Nancy nodded and followed the woman downstairs to a long black car with smoked glass windows and a silver statuette of Diana on the hood. *It suits its owner well,* Nancy thought. *Like a modern broomstick.*

As the witch threaded her way through the traffic, Nancy tried to look back inconspicuously. Since she did not know what kind of car Ned had rented, she could not tell for sure whether the green Datsun she glimpsed now and then was her friend's. She hoped desperately that it was!

Soon they had reached a desolate area of abandoned warehouses near the Hudson River. Nancy became frightened. The woman had not gone to the cemetery! If Ned was not right behind them, he would never find her!

Madame Arnette stopped the car. "Here's where we get out," she announced.

"But you said—"

"I am going by the aura," the witch replied. "My feeling tells me that this is the place. Come with me!"

She led Nancy to an empty warehouse. *No way I'm going in there,* the girl detective said to herself. But before Madame Arnette could open the door, it was pushed out by a man who instantly grabbed the girl. *He was Ponsonby, the detective!*

Nancy screamed, fighting and kicking, but between the two of them, her enemies had her subdued in a moment.

"So much for you, young lady!" the detective sneered. "You won't make any more trouble for us. We'll see to that!"

"No Linda Brown was buried at Saint Barbara's,"

Madame Arnette put in. "We also checked on you and found out you're a detective!"

Ponsonby tied Nancy's hands and feet with a thick rope, while Madame Arnette went on, "You've been spying on us! Well, you'll see what happens to someone who tries to trick Diana's priestess!"

While Nancy looked on helplessly, the witch and Ponsonby grabbed large cannisters from a shelf near the door and poured a trail of gasoline along the walls of the rickety old building. As soon as they lighted the gas, flames shot up, licking the dry wood and gradually catching the deteriorating boards.

The two criminals had left a large enough area around the door to insure their retreat. "You'll be a sacrifice to Diana!" Madame Arnette shouted as they hurried outside. "Good-bye, Nancy Drew!"

A moment later, Nancy heard nothing but the crackling, burning wood around her. Feverishly, she tugged on her bonds and screamed for help. The fire was spreading fast. If no one heard her within the next few minutes, it would engulf her completely!

Smoke was already scratching her nostrils, and tears streamed from her eyes. Her bonds, rather than giving way, cut deeper and deeper into her wrists.

Suddenly, the door was flung open. "I'm coming, Nancy!" Ned yelled. "Hold on just one more second!"

He whipped out his pocket knife and freed the girl, then he pulled her up. "Come on. Hurry."

He dragged the choking girl out the door, barely escaping the fire, which had worked itself closer and closer to the frame. A moment later, part of the old structure fell in with a thundering crash. Flames pierced the night sky as Ned and Nancy ran away from the inferno to Ned's rented green Datsun.

"I got stuck in traffic!" Ned explained after they were safely in the car, and he had started the engine. "Luckily, I saw the black limousine when I came down this street. I thought that's where you had gone, but I wasn't really sure until I recognized that Diana ornament on the hood."

Just then they heard a bell clanging in the distance. Firemen, alerted by the blaze, were rushing toward the scene.

Ned cut the engine. "We might as well stay and tell them what happened," he said. "I just hope they believe us and don't suspect us of starting the fire."

Nancy nodded, wiping her tears. A moment later the two were talking to the fire chief. "Nancy Drew?" he asked. "Seems I've heard that name before. Aren't you the famous girl detective?"

"Yes," Nancy replied and rubbed her sore wrist. Then she told her story.

"My aunt, Eloise Drew, will confirm that I left her apartment with Madame Arnette tonight," the girl concluded. "And I don't really want to alert the police until I can spring a trap on that woman. If she gets scared away, I may never be able to prove her scheme!"

"How long do you think you'll need?" the fire chief inquired. "We have to make a report, you know."

Nancy nodded. "I understand. But I believe that I can expose the witch if I drop in on her meeting, which should have started by now."

"Okay," the fire chief said. "It will take us some time to get things under control here, anyway. Good luck!"

When Nancy and Ned returned to the apartment, Aunt Eloise told her that the coven had, indeed, assembled and that the chanting had stopped only a few moments ago.

"Good," Nancy exclaimed. "That means Madame Arnette is going into her trance. Here's my chance!"

She ran to the balcony door, then turned around. "Ned, please call the police and tell them to come over right away!" A moment later, she was gone. She made her way to Madame Arnette's bedroom, opened the unlocked window, and climbed in. Silently, she tiptoed to the bureau and pulled out the witch's green notebook. On the first page, she saw the entry she was looking for. "Need more information about Nancy Drew."

Nancy quickly leafed through the rest of the ledger and realized it contained personal notes on members of the coven and their dead relatives, obviously all the result of Ponsonby's investigations.

Nancy closed the book and turned to leave, when she noted something odd on one wall. A hole was stuffed with green, crinkled paper, the kind used for decorations. In front of it stood a lamp with a powerful electric bulb.

The open-mouthed sphinx must be on the other side, Nancy said to herself. *It produces an eerie green glow when the light is on.*

Quickly, she examined the hole and found a tube concealed in the paper. *Aha,* Nancy thought. *Someone stands here and speaks in Diana's unearthly voice! I'm sure the members of the coven will be surprised when they see this.*

Next to the lamp on the table lay a piece of paper with this evening's script. It was hand-written on personal stationery with the name Christina Egmont in the upper left corner!

Nancy gasped in surprise. Then she took a deep breath, and with a pounding heart, opened the door to the living room. There, the high priestess, bathed in moonlight, was in the middle of her trance act, intoning a prediction to one of the women.

Nancy found a switch next to the door and turned on the light. Madame Arnette stared at her, open-mouthed, while the members of the coven cried out in surprise.

The young detective held up the green notebook. She read an excerpt, consisting of Mrs. Hughes's communication with her husband at the last meeting. "This information was supplied to Madame Arnette by a detective named Ponsonby," she explained. "He and the high priestess tied me up in a warehouse earlier tonight and set it on fire. They wanted to kill me because I was on to their scheme!"

The women sat, frozen in shock, and the head witch, no longer wrapped in moonlight and mystery, looked panic-stricken.

"If you'll all come into the bedroom," Nancy went on, "I'll show you a hole stuffed with green paper and a lamp in front of it. Madame Arnette's neighbor, Christina Egmont, an actress, plays Diana for you at these meetings."

Suddenly, the women came back to life. They

shouted furiously, some running into the bedroom to see the evidence, others crowding around Madame Arnette, accusing her of lying to them. "We want our money back!" A tall, heavyset woman cried out, "You're not going to get away with this!"

Just then the bell rang. Nancy opened the door and admitted two police officers, followed by Ned and Aunt Eloise. To Nancy's surprise, Mrs. Egmont appeared a moment later. She had heard the commotion and had come to find out what was going on. As soon as she saw the police, however, she turned on her heels and tried to run.

"Stop that woman!" Nancy cried. "She's in on this scheme!"

When one of the officers brought the actress into the room, Mrs. Egmont acted indignant. "What is this all about?" she demanded. "Why are you holding me?"

"Because you played Diana," Nancy told her. "Your training enabled you to project your voice and sound convincing. When you were finished, you retreated to your apartment over the balcony. And to divert any suspicion from yourself, you complained to my aunt about the noises in here. Very clever!"

"You can't prove a thing!" Mrs. Egmont snapped. "It's all conjecture."

Nancy smiled. "It would have been if you hadn't left your script, written on your letterhead!"

Mrs. Egmont's mouth dropped open and she did not say another word. When the police had led the two women away, the rest of the coven began to leave. Many thanked Nancy for exposing the fraud, and Mrs. Hughes gave the girl a big hug.

"I was such a fool," she sobbed. "I spent all my savings to be able to talk to my husband . . . " Her voice trailed off.

"I'm sure most of the money will be found in Madame Arnette's bank account," Nancy said, "and be refunded."

"I'm glad that evil woman can't continue her dishonest game," Ned added. "Nancy, you did a wonderful job!"

An impish smile crossed Nancy's face. "I guess the moral is: be careful what you write in your notebook. It may come back to haunt you!"

THE PHANTOM
OF ROOM 513

Pretty, titian-haired Nancy Drew clutched her right side and took a deep breath as the electronic doors of Rosemont Hospital swung open. "Dad, don't worry," she said to Carson Drew. "I'm sure I'm fine."

"Just the same," her father replied, "I'll feel better when the *doctor* says you're fine. This is no ordinary stomach ache!"

They walked into the brightly lit emergency room. A nurse in a crisp white uniform and stiff white cap approached them. "Can I help you?" she asked Nancy, noticing the girl's pale, drawn face.

"My side hurts," Nancy replied.

"Follow me," the nurse said, leading them to an examining room. What's your name?"

"Nancy Drew. This is my father, Carson Drew."

The nurse nodded. "Mr. Drew, would you go to the front desk and fill out some papers? After that, please

113

take a seat in the waiting room. We'll call you when your daughter's been examined." Then she disappeared through a door in the back of the small room.

"Guess what?" Nancy heard the nurse say to someone. "We have the famous girl detective here, with a pain in her right side. What do you want to bet that she has appendicitis? And the only available room is haunted!"

"I know," a man replied. "The goings-on in that room are strange, all right. I never believed in ghosts before, but Room 513 is something else! What really bothers me is that Edinburgh is the surgeon on call. I don't like the idea of having him operate on her. I hear Nancy Drew is a fine young lady, and she deserves better than that. But so do all the patients."

"Shh," the nurse hissed. "You'll get us all in trouble."

A young, dark-haired man in a white jacket walked in. "Miss Drew," he said, "I'm Dr. Daniels. If you'll lie down, I'll examine you. The nurse told me you have pain in your right side. Have you ever had trouble with your appendix?" As he spoke, he wrapped a blood pressure cuff around her arm.

"No," she said, then paused. "Doctor Daniels, did I hear the nurse say that one of the hospital rooms is haunted?"

"Haunted? I should think not! You don't believe in ghosts, do you, Nancy?"

Nancy was confused. She could see that the doctor did not want to discuss hospital ghosts. But he was the man whose voice she had heard before!

114

"Do you really think it's my appendix?" she asked. She had a date with her boyfriend, Ned Nickerson, that weekend!

The doctor gently poked at her abdomen. "Does this hurt?" he asked.

"A little."

"We'll have to do some tests," he went on. "It may turn out to be nothing."

He continued to examine her, then a nurse came in to take a blood sample. While Nancy was waiting for the results, another nurse entered the room.

"Lisa!" Nancy cried, delighted to see her friend Lisa Scotti, who had shared an adventure with her in *The Swami's Ring.*

"Hi, Nancy," Lisa said and hugged the young detective. "I just found out the problem is not your appendix. They don't really know what it is, so they want to keep you here and do some tests."

Nancy nodded. "It really hurts."

"I'm going to give you something for the pain as soon as we get you checked into a room. It'll also make you sleep so you'll feel better in the morning."

"Does my dad know?" Nancy asked while Lisa gave her an injection.

"Yes. I told him. He wanted to come in to say goodnight, but I discouraged him so you could get some rest. He said he'll call you in the morning."

"Are you going to put me in that haunted room?"

"Of course not. We'll find you another one. Dr. Daniels is working on that right now."

"Tell me what's going on."

"I will, tomorrow. Maybe you could even—"

Nancy giggled. "Check it out, you mean?"

"Well, this may be our opportunity to get rid of the ghost," Lisa replied. "With you around, he doesn't have much of a chance!"

"I'm looking forward to meeting the ghost," Nancy said.

About twenty minutes later, Nancy was in her hospital room resting. But despite the medication the young nurse had given her, Nancy woke up in the middle of the night. The room was small, and some light filtered in from the hallway, through the slightly opened door. There were two beds in the room, and a gray-haired lady was snoring peacefully next to Nancy.

Just then, the girl heard loud thumping. She looked around to see if something had fallen. Everything was still. Eerie. Nancy pulled herself up to rest on her elbows.

The thumps grew louder, turning into crashing noises, and then she heard a woman's pitiful moaning. Though she couldn't make out any distinct words, it sounded as if the poor woman was in terrible distress.

Nancy blinked her eyes. She was still sleepy, and wondered for a moment if she were dreaming.

"Help me! Help me!" the voice wailed.

Nancy sat up straighter. Her roommate opened her eyes. "Who are you? What are you doing in my room?" she asked the young detective.

"My name is Nancy Drew. I'm going to have some tests done tomorrow."

"This is a private room," the woman grumbled. "Oh

well, maybe there wasn't any other place to put you. I wish that racket out there would stop. It's hard to sleep here."

"Is a patient making all that noise?" Nancy asked.

"No, it's the ghost," the woman answered.

Nancy closed her eyes and lay back. Ghost or no ghost, her stomach still hurt somewhat, and she was sleepy.

When she awoke again, sunlight was pouring in through the window. Lisa walked in with a breakfast tray. She put it down in front of the gray-haired woman, who sat up.

"I'm sorry if I was grouchy last night," she said to Nancy. "I'm Mabel Greenfield. There's so much commotion here at night, it's hard to get any rest. They took out my gall bladder two weeks ago, and I don't feel any better than I did then. I don't know what to think about that doctor of mine."

"Who's your doctor?" Nancy inquired.

"Dr. Edinburgh," the woman replied.

Nancy frowned. No one had voiced much confidence in this doctor.

Later on that morning, Bess Marvin and George Fayne came to visit their friend.

"Nancy, I can't believe you're in the hospital!" tall, dark-haired George exclaimed. She assumed a theatrical pose and gazed into the distance. "And she was so young."

"Cut it out, George," Nancy said. "My stomach still hurts when I laugh. By the way, look who's here!"

117

"Lisa!" George and Bess cried in unison when the young nurse, who had been rolling up Mrs. Greenfield's bed, turned around. "It's good to see you."

Lisa smiled. "Keep talking to Nancy," she said. "She's been down in the dumps ever since she missed breakfast this morning."

"Why can't I have anything to eat?" the young detective asked.

"You can, as soon as we've done your tests. They must be done on an empty stomach."

Nancy groaned. "I'm starved. And I do feel better."

"Good," Lisa said matter-of-factly. "Now, do you want to hear about the haunted room?"

"Haunted room?" Bess stared at her.

"A very sick woman was in there," the nurse explained. "She disappeared without a trace. The police have searched, but no one knows what happened to her."

"Don't they have any clues?" Nancy asked.

"There's a rumor," Lisa continued, "that her husband killed her. It's just a rumor; there's no proof that she's even dead."

Mrs. Greenfield joined in on the conversation. "Lisa says that there's no proof. But you heard those moans last night. That was her. She often comes back to the scene of the crime, and sometimes she calls her husband's name. Yes, she calls for Harold. I've heard people say that things move in there by themselves, and she floats around all purple and ghostly looking! Some nights she begs him not to hurt her. Yes, she's dead all right. And her husband is off the hook for what he did!"

"You may be right, Mrs. Greenfield," Lisa said. "But we don't know for sure. The police have questioned him, and all they learned was that he and his wife had big life insurance policies on each other. But he hasn't tried to collect on it." She turned to Nancy.

"It would help so much if you could figure all this out, once you feel better. Patients get scared when the moaning starts."

"I haven't seen anything about it in the newspapers," George said.

"They've kept it hush-hush," Lisa explained.

"If you ask me," Mrs. Greenfield said, "it's because of those doctors. They have the money to keep it quiet. That's why that doctor's brother got away with murder!"

"Doctor's brother?" Nancy asked.

"The missing woman," Lisa said, "was Lilith Edinburgh. Her husband was, supposedly, the surgeon's brother."

"Curious," Nancy said. "The same names keep popping up. Why was Lilith Edinburgh in the hospital?"

"Unspecified ailment," Lisa replied. "We were running a wide spectrum of tests on her."

"Was there a sign of struggle in the room?"

Lisa Scotti shook her head. "One day she was there, the next, she was gone. No one knows anything."

"It doesn't add up," Nancy said. "If her husband wanted to do anything to her, why do it at the hospital, where he would risk being seen. Have the police examined the room?"

"Thoroughly," Lisa said. "They didn't find anything."

"How long ago did this happen?"

"Several months ago," Lisa answered. "The 'ghost' only appears now and then. We haven't put anyone in the room since a young tonsilitis patient screamed in the middle of the night. She said she saw Lilith Edinburgh."

"What kind of doctor is this Dr. Edinburgh?" Nancy asked. "Is he really as bad as everyone keeps saying?"

Lisa looked down at the floor. "That's a tricky question. He used to be an excellent, conscientious surgeon. But then something happened to him. He became—strange. He even looks different now."

"Is he sued for malpractice often?" Nancy asked.

"If I don't get better soon, *I'll* sue him!" Mrs. Greenfield grumbled. "I was in better shape before he took my gall bladder out!"

"But, Mrs. Greenfield," Lisa said, "according to your chart, you're improving rapidly!"

"But I feel horrible!" the woman insisted.

"I'll write a special note on your chart," Lisa said. "And I'll tell the doctor. Nancy, in answer to your question, he rarely gets sued. People have complained, but they always back off. Now I'd better take a look at Mrs. Greenfield."

She drew the curtain that divided the two beds. Just then a man in a white jacket walked into the room.

"Oh, good morning, Dr. Edinburgh," Lisa said. "I was just going to examine Mrs. Greenfield."

"I'll take care of that," the doctor said, and disappeared behind the drawn curtain. Lisa waved to the girls and left, and George and Bess stood up.

"We'd better go," George said to Nancy. "We'll call you later."

While the doctor was examining her roommate, Nancy took a piece of paper and a pencil from her night table and drew a sketch of the surgeon. She covered it when he rose to leave, and took another look at him. *I think I captured his features fairly well,* the girl thought, then put the sketch in her drawer.

A moment later, Lisa came in again. She looked at Mrs. Greenfield's chart. "Everything seems to be fine," she said.

"Well, it isn't," the woman complained. "But the doctor doesn't seem to be worried. He didn't even examine me properly!"

Lisa hesitated for a moment, then said, "Let me take a look." A few minutes later, she opened the curtain.

"May I tell my friend what I found?" she asked Mrs. Greenfield.

"Please go ahead," the woman replied. "Maybe it'll help."

Lisa frowned. "Nancy, I don't understand. According to the chart, there is no sign of infection. No fever, swelling, or redness are indicated. But her upper right abdomen, where she had the surgery, is swollen and red and infected. This poor woman must be in a lot of pain. She's hardly been able to eat. And Dr. Edinburgh didn't even note it. Something's wrong here. I'll have to report it!"

"Lisa, is there someone you can trust to take care of Mrs. Greenfield, without reporting Dr. Edinburgh just yet? I'll need one more day."

"Sure. What do you have in mind?"

Nancy pulled out her sketch of the doctor. "Do you think someone else would recognize him from this?"

Lisa shrugged. "Well, you're a better detective than you are an artist, but this is quite a good rendering. But tell me—"

"I have an idea," Nancy said. "Let me call Bess and George. I'll need their help."

That night, Nancy stood in her room and scanned the hallway. She felt much better, and so far none of the tests indicated any problem. Lisa had told her that there were few nurses working the late shift, so that would be the best time for Nancy to investigate.

The young detective wrapped her blue robe around her and tiptoed down the hallway to Room 513, making sure no one saw her. Gingerly, she opened the door. A gust of air hit her in the face.

She tried to turn on the light, but to no avail. She looked at the window across the room. It appeared to be shut! Where had the cold air come from?

Her arms broke out in goosebumps as the room was filled with an unearthly wailing.

"Ohhh, ohhh, helllp meeee!" the eerie voice moaned. "Haaaarooollld, ohhh, Harrooolld! Hellllp! Don't hurrrrrt meee!"

In the dim light filtering in through the hallway, Nancy looked around the room. There was nothing but an empty unmade bed, a bedside table, and a chair.

The gusts began again, wildly blowing her hair and filling her ears with its hollow noise.

When her eyes had adjusted to the scarce light, she walked to the window and felt it. It was closed securely!

All at once, a haze of purple lights appeared in the center of the room. They wove in and out of grotesque shapes, then took the form of a woman, much larger than life.

"Hellp! Helllp!" the screeching continued, and chills ran up Nancy's spine.

Suddenly, she heard the thud of approaching footsteps. She backed into a closet just before the door opened.

She crouched in the corner holding her breath. The closet door was open a few inches. As she pressed against the wall to avoid being seen, she felt it give way slightly.

Nancy stared through the crack in the door. Dr. Edinburgh had entered the room, and the ghost of Lilith Edinburgh wove around him.

"Hello, Lilith," he said, chuckling. "What brought you out to play tonight?"

"Helllp meeee," the ghost wailed.

"You need some rest," the doctor said, as the figure appeared to move right through him! "We'll visit some other time."

He left the room, gently shutting the door behind him. The ghost immediately disappeared!

Nancy groped to see if the closet had a light. She found a switch and flicked it. To her relief, it worked.

She examined the wall behind her and found a panel that slid aside, revealing a small room. A student chair with an attached desk top stood in the middle of it, and on it were two stacks of hospital charts.

Nancy sat down and quickly read through the first few charts on each pile. One seemed to contain accounts of patients whose health had improved as a result of surgery by Dr. Edinburgh. Among them was the chart for Mrs. Greenfield. The second stack contained records of people who had developed complications after surgery.

Strange, Nancy said to herself. *I wonder if Dr. Edinburgh took those charts out of the general file to fix them so all his patients show improvement. Maybe he's already worked on one of the stacks, but not on the other!*

She slipped out of the closet and headed back to her room, anxious to talk to Lisa in the morning. She thought about Bess and George, hoping they had been successful in their mission. Then she went to sleep. It had been a long, tiring day for her.

George and Bess had been waiting in the Faynes' station wagon near the back door of the hospital. The entrance was brightly lit and they watched the door intently.

After about thirty minutes, a man in a white jacket and gray slacks walked out.

"That's him!" Bess said excitedly. "He looks just like the picture Nancy drew!"

George nodded as they watched the man hurry to a red Buick.

As Edinburgh drove out of the parking lot, George switched on her headlights and followed. The Buick turned onto the tree-lined avenue leading from the hospital, and the girls stayed far enough behind so the doctor would not notice them.

After a while, Edinburgh turned right. Bess looked at the crumpled paper she had in her hand. "He's not going home," she declared. "He lives on Woodlawn Avenue, but he's heading in the opposite direction!"

Soon they were driving into the countryside, where the houses were spaced far apart. There were no street lights on the narrow road they turned into, and the full moon cast weird shadows from the trees.

"I'm getting nervous," Bess said. "Maybe we should go back."

"No," George declared. "Nancy asked us to follow this guy, and that's what we'll do." Dust billowed from the street as the two continued their surveillance.

Finally, Dr. Edinburgh stopped in front of a small house.

George immediately turned off the lights and pulled over to the side of the road. Suddenly, she felt her left front wheel drop down into a ditch.

"Oh, no!" Bess moaned.

"Shh!" George said and quickly turned off the engine. The girls watched the man enter the house, then George started the car up again and tried to move it. It would not budge!

"What'll we do!" Bess whispered in fear. "Now we're stuck!"

"We'll worry about it later," George decided. "First let's have a look at that house and see what our good doctor is up to."

Not giving her cousin a chance to object, she got out of the car and walked up to the little house. Bess followed reluctantly. They stopped in front of a brightly lit window.

Inside, Dr. Edinburgh took off his white jacket. He was laughing and chatting with a woman.

"Poor Harold!" they heard the woman say. "What are you planning to do with him?"

Dr. Edinburgh shrugged. "Don't worry about it. I've got plans for him. He tried to meddle in my business and deserves everything he gets."

The woman poured a glass of orange juice. "I guess it serves him right. He was willing to call the police on you. Now he's getting a dose of his own medicine. And you're getting richer."

"And so are you, Lilith," Dr. Edinburgh said. "I haven't forgotten your cut of the money. I was willing to cut Harold in, too, when he found out what I had pulled in Chicago. Remember how mad he got when I offered him a trip around the world?"

"Yes, I do," she replied. "But I'm ready to take you up on it. I'm tired of having him stand in my way, keeping me from doing exciting things!"

Bess and George exchanged a sharp glance.

"He called her Lilith!" George whispered. "That's the missing woman!"

"That's right!" Bess said. The girls were so excited by

their discovery that they paid no attention to the two people in the house for several moments. Then they heard a noise behind them and whirled around. They gasped when the doctor shone a bright flashlight into their faces!

The morning sun poured through the hospital window as Lisa poked her head into Nancy's room. "How are you doing this morning?" she asked in a cheery voice. "It looks like you ate well!" she added, as she noticed Nancy's empty plate.

"I feel great!" Nancy said. "Breakfast was fabulous, and it's a beautiful day. Besides, I found some clues last night! Sit down, and I'll tell you about them while Mrs. Greenfield is in the shower."

"I'm all ears," Lisa replied, straightening her pert white nurse's cap. She sat on the edge of Nancy's hospital bed.

"I went into the haunted room," Nancy said. "I saw the ghost—or whatever it is. Dr. Edinburgh was *talking* to it! I also saw stacks of hospital charts. They were hidden in the closet."

"What!" Lisa exclaimed. "I can't imagine why charts would be in that room. Did you look at any of them?"

"Yes. Do you remember a patient named George Knipp? His was one of the charts I read. Something struck me as odd. Would you mind describing his condition when he was in the hospital? It says he was discharged a few days ago."

Lisa's expression grew serious. "That was another one of Dr. Edinburgh's sad cases. He took out the man's gall bladder." She lowered her voice. "Between you and me, I don't think the man needed the surgery. But Dr. Edinburgh operated, and Mr. Knipp became terribly sick afterward. All kinds of complications set in. He had a raging infection, his blood pressure was too low, and his pulse was weak. He finally recovered, but he'll never be as strong and healthy as he was before surgery."

Nancy's blue eyes flashed. "The chart says that he did fine after the operation!"

"It couldn't," Lisa said. "I did some of the charting myself!"

Nancy nodded her head. "I know. Your name is signed in several places! But Edinburgh falsified the information."

Mrs. Greenfield walked back into the room. "Good morning, Nurse!" she said to Lisa. "It's so nice to see you young people chatting. Well, don't let me interrupt. You just go on talking. Being in the same room with Nancy has made me feel young myself!"

The detective blushed. "Mrs. Greenfield has been so nice," she said. "Lisa, if Mr. Knipp had such a hard recovery, did he sue the doctor?"

"That poor Mr. Knipp!" Mrs. Greenfield exclaimed. "Oh, he wanted to sue all right. He should have, if you ask me. Changed his mind at the last minute. I knew he should have used a different lawyer. If only I'd known him before I let Dr. Edinburgh operate on me!"

"What do you mean?" Nancy asked.

"I hear that there's a lawyer named Melvin Smith who takes malpractice cases," Mrs. Greenfield replied, "but lots of times, he talks his clients out of suing. Says they don't have a good enough case. If you ask me, that doctor paid him to prevent the lawsuit!"

Just then, Bess and George entered the room. "I was about to call you," Nancy said. "I was starting to worry!"

"With good reason!" Bess said.

"He saw us," George told Nancy. "He caught us hiding in the trees outside his lake cabin. Did we have some fancy talking to do!"

"Go on!" Nancy urged. She explained to Mrs. Greenfield that the cousins had followed Dr. Edinburgh the night before.

"He didn't go to his home," George continued. "He went to a little house outside of town. A woman was there, and he called her Lilith!"

"Lilith Edinburgh!" the others echoed.

George nodded and repeated the conversation the cousins had overheard. "And then he caught us," she finished.

"What happened?" Nancy asked.

"Well," George said, "we were lucky. When we got there, I turned my lights off and pulled to the side of the road. Our car got stuck. It worked in our favor, because when Edinburgh saw us, we told him we were looking for help."

"He came to the car with us and pushed us out!" Bess added with a chuckle.

"I still don't understand," Mrs. Greenfield said. "Lilith Edinburgh is alive? Then how is her ghost haunting the hospital?"

"I have a hunch, but I need to prove it," Nancy said. "Let me call my father. He may be able to help."

It was night again, and the fifth floor of Rosemont Hospital was quiet. Almost all the patients were asleep and the visitors had gone home. Only Nancy was wide awake. She and Lisa crept down the deserted hall, while George and Bess waited in the room with Mrs. Greenfield.

Cautiously, Nancy opened the door to Room 513. She flicked the light switch, but the place remained pitch black. Moans began again, just like the previous night. "Hellllp meeee!" the ghostly voice screeched and gusts of cold air blew the girls' hair!

Purple and yellow lights floated in the middle of the room. They weaved and danced and took on the form of a huge, shadowy woman.

"Oh, no!" Lisa gasped. "It is a ghost!"

"I wonder," Nancy said. She flicked the switch once again. The moaning stopped, and the lights disappeared.

"I don't believe it!" Lisa whispered.

"Watch," Nancy said, and flicked the switch a third time. Nothing happened. On the fifth flick, the ghost appeared again.

"Every now and then it comes when you turn the switch," Nancy told Lisa. "Did you bring the flashlight?"

"I sure did." The young nurse pulled a tiny flashlight from the big pocket in her uniform. Nancy took it and shone it around the room until she found the chair she

131

remembered. She pulled it up under the light, stepped up on it, and began to unscrew the fixture.

"Lisa, shine the beam up here. Look! There's a hologram projector hidden in the fixture. It creates the lights. And there's a tiny tape recorder, wired into the electrical system. Sometimes, when you flick the switch, the lights don't work, but the ghost is turned on. The intervals are irregular, to make it more real. Very clever!"

Lisa flashed her light around the room. "Nancy!" she cried, "there's a fan in the corner. That must make the wind gusts."

"Let's go see the charts," Nancy said as she climbed down from the chair. The girls walked to the closet and opened the door. Then they froze in fright!

"Not so fast!" Dr. Edinburgh sneered as he grabbed both Nancy and Lisa by their arms. "Your snooping days are over, Nancy Drew! You should have been content to remain a patient!"

Just then, a voice boomed out behind them. "Her snooping days aren't over, Edinburgh!" Mr. Drew shouted. He looked over his shoulder. "Take him, officer," he said, and a policeman snapped handcuffs on the man.

The following day, Mr. Drew, Bess, and George came to take Nancy home from the hospital. The tests had proved negative, and her condition had been diagnosed as a spastic colon, which was very painful but of no consequence.

"Nancy!" George cried out when she entered the room. "You have to tell us what's been going on!"

"I hear you caught Dr. Edinburgh," Bess added.

"Yes, except that he *wasn't* Dr. Edinburgh," Nancy said.

"What!"

"He was the doctor's identical twin brother, Jim. Jim had been a medic in the army. He'd been in trouble with the law, and Harold Edinburgh, the older twin, threatened to expose him. So he had to disappear."

"But he didn't really," Mr. Drew went on. "He kidnapped his brother and posed as Dr. Edinburgh. He did a lot of surgery, and made plenty of money. But he didn't have the necessary skills, and many patients developed complications after their operations. That's why Jim Edinburgh falsified their charts. He worked with a crooked lawyer, Melvin Smith, who talked Edinburgh's patients out of suing him. Smith was arrested this morning."

"But what about the ghost?" Bess asked.

"Well, Jim Edinburgh's sister-in-law was no longer happy being married to her husband Harold and wanted to leave him, but she knew he would never let her go," Nancy took up the story. "So Jim arranged for Lilith to disappear. After the police investigated the hospital, he fixed the wiring in Room 513 and rigged up the ghost. This way, people would believe Lilith had really died. Plus, it would scare people away so Jim could work on the charts in private."

"But what about the real Doctor Edinburgh?" George interjected. "Where is he now?"

Nancy went on to explain that his brother had kept the doctor locked in the basement of a small house on

133

the outskirts of town, with no way of escaping. The police had found him that morning a bit shaken up, but not hurt.

Just then the phone rang. Nancy picked up the receiver and heard the voice of Ned Nickerson, her boyfriend, on the other end.

"Hi, there," he said. "We had a date last night. Or did you forget?"

"Oh, Ned!" she cried. "I'm sorry. Let me explain."

Ned chuckled. "You don't have to. Your dad told me everything. I just wanted to tell you that I'm glad you're feeling better. And Nancy, as far as our date is concerned, don't worry. I know I could never compete with a ghost!"

FOREST
OF FEAR

Nancy Drew pulled her blue sports sedan up to a fork of the wooded, dirt road.

"This looks like the way to Lake Oolagah," she told her friends, Bess Marvin and George Fayne.

"But where is the sign that used to be here?" tall, dark-haired George asked.

"Yes," Bess added and pointed. "All I see is that weird-looking thing."

In place of the Lake Oolagah sign was a crudely drawn skull and crossbones nailed to a tree.

"Maybe the lake's closed now," George said. "It *has* been several years since we've been here."

"If that were the case, the government would have blocked off the road," Nancy said, and continued along the dusty path while the sun was rapidly setting behind the treetops.

A few minutes later they passed another crude sign. "Danger—Go back!" it read.

Bess became worried. "Let's turn around," she said. "See how barren the trees are? Something's wrong here."

"I know," Nancy said. "But I'd like to know what it is."

The farther they drove, the less living vegetation there was. The trees and bushes, which should have been bursting with new shoots and leaves, were dead, skeletal things that seemed to be reaching ominously for the car. And darkness was descending rapidly, stretching long shadows across the roadway.

"This is getting spooky," Bess shuddered. "Let's go back."

"Not until we find out what this is all about," Nancy said. "The lake should be less than a mile from here."

They pushed on. Far off the roadside they saw a makeshift cabin of odd-sized planks and rocks. Nancy did not remember it being there before. Dead, rotting trees surrounded it like a natural fence. She wondered what kind of person would put a house in the middle of such desolation.

"There's the lake!" Bess said, pointing. The road went right up to a small spillway for unloading boats into the water.

"Strange," Nancy said. "It looks like Lake Oolagah, but—"

Bess frowned. "It's as if it got old and died," she added.

"Died is right," George murmured and got out of the

car. She walked to the water's edge. "Look at this."
Nancy and Bess joined her and stared. The ground on
the shore was littered with fish skeletons!

"What happened here?" George asked.

Nancy surveyed the countryside. The lake covered
about twelve acres, which gave her a good view of the
surrounding forest. It was all dead!

"I have no idea," she said.

"What should we do?" George asked. "It's getting
dark."

"And we haven't had dinner yet," Bess interjected.

Nancy smiled at her. "Just keep thinking how good
you'll look at the Spring Fling if you skip dinner."

Bess looked horrified. "Bite your tongue!"

The girls laughed. "I suggest we set up camp anyway," Nancy said, "then worry about what to do in the
morning."

Bess and George agreed, and in the last light of the
fading sun, they hurried to unload the tent and sleeping bags from the car.

"Okay," Nancy said, surveying the gear on the
ground. "Let's get—"

"Nancy!" Bess screamed, her face white as milk.
"There—in the trees!"

They looked up. A canteen dropped from George's
hand and clattered loudly to the ground. Large, glow-
ing orbs moved lazily through the parched woods!

There were four of them, then a fifth. They glowed a
warm yellow as they flitted through the spindly trees—
the only things that seemed alive in the deserted forest.

"What do you think that is?" George asked.

"G-ghosts!" Bess whispered, her throat dry.

"Bess!" Nancy snapped.

"What else could it be?" Bess replied. "Look at them, waltzing around there. What if they come down here?"

"Then maybe we'd get some idea of what they really are," Nancy returned.

The ghost lights moved through the woods for several frightening minutes, then, all at once, they began to rise. Slowly at first, then more rapidly, the eerie orbs floated up into the night sky to dwindle, then disappear into the darkness.

Bess leaned against the fender of the car. "Whew," she breathed. "I've never been so scared in my whole life."

"Neither have I," George confessed.

She walked to the passenger side of the car and opened the door. "Let's go," she said. "We've had enough excitement for one night."

"What about the gear?" Nancy asked.

"No one will take it," George said, climbing into the back seat through the driver's door. "Let's find a motel. We'll come back for the stuff in the morning."

Nancy was reluctant to leave the camping equipment behind, but Bess and George were so frightened that she got into the car.

As she drove, her friends recalled frightening experiences in the past, frequent occurrences when they helped Nancy in her detective work.

Suddenly George sat up straight. "I don't recognize this road," she said. "Did we make the wrong turn?"

"We might have," Nancy admitted. "It's so dark I can hardly see where I'm going."

"What's that sound?" Bess asked.

A loud rumbling noise seemed to be drawing nearer to them.

"I don't know," Nancy began. "I—"

The next moment, piercing beams of light were blinding them.

"It's a truck!" George exclaimed. "Why doesn't it turn off its brights?"

As if in answer to her question, the truck dimmed its lights as it prepared to pass them from the opposite direction.

"What's a big truck like that doing way out here?" Nancy asked. "This isn't near any highway."

The truck slowed and rumbled past them on the narrow, tree-lined road. It was a large white tanker with the words Dunbar Enterprises printed in red on the side. The driver, barely visible in his cab, honked and waved good-naturedly as he drove by.

"Maybe we should turn around and retrace our route," George said.

"There are lights up ahead," Nancy replied. "Let's see what they are, first."

They followed the forest road until it led them to a large industrial complex. A big wire fence with Dunbar Enterprises written on it prevented them from going farther.

Nancy stopped in front of the gate, and a security guard came out to the car.

"Evenin' girls," he said. "What can I do for you?"

"We're lost," Nancy said.

"And hungry," Bess added.

"Can you tell us how to get to the nearest motel?" George asked.

The man grinned. "Took the wrong road, huh," he said, shaking his head. "Happens all the time. What you do is go back the way you came and take the first left. Lutherville is about five miles away."

"You sure are located in the middle of nowhere," Nancy told the man.

He shrugged. "We used to have a big old plant in Cleveland," he said. "Then Mr. Dunbar decided to build a new, ultra-modern factory out here and relocate everybody. I come from the country anyhow, so it was a good move for me."

"What do you make?" Bess asked.

"Toys!" the man explained. "All kinds of plastic toys."

Just then, a delivery truck pulled up behind Nancy's car and honked.

"Whoops," the guard said. "I'd better get back to work."

The girls waved to the pleasant man as Nancy turned around and headed toward Lutherville.

They found the town within fifteen minutes, though a good section of it was boarded up and deserted. Only one motel, the Rest-a-Spell, seemed to be open. They pulled up to the manager's office and went in.

A bell rang when they opened the door and a small,

gray-haired lady came in from the living area in back of the office.

"Pretty late for you young ladies to be out," she said, and smiled. "I'm Mrs. Johnson. We don't get too many guests here anymore."

"I'm Nancy Drew," Nancy said. "And these are my friends, Bess Marvin and George Fayne."

"George?" the woman said, wrinkling her nose. "Funny name for a girl."

"We were going to camp out at Lake Oolagah," Nancy said, "but—"

"Don't say any more," Mrs. Johnson interrupted. "The reason Lutherville looks like a ghost town is because of that lake."

"What happened?" George asked.

The woman frowned. "One room with two big beds okay?" she asked.

The girls nodded.

She pulled a key from a pegboard. "Come on. We'll chat on the way."

They left the office and walked down a line of small cottages, stopping in front of number nine. "This is the nicest one I have," Mrs. Johnson said and opened the door to a pleasant, colonial-style room.

"Now, you want to know about the lake?" she asked as the girls walked past her. "It's ghosts!"

"I told you!" Bess said, throwing herself on one of the beds. "Are there any restaurants open this late?"

Mrs. Johnson shook her head. "I can whip up a few cheeseburgers, though, and put them on the bill."

143

"Sounds like heaven." Bess sighed.

"What about Lake Oolagah?" Nancy persisted.

"An old Indian came into town a couple of years ago," the old woman said sadly. "His name was John Bearcloud. He went around telling everyone that the lake and surrounding area was an old Delaware Indian burial ground and that we were all cursed for desecrating it. He built a lean-to out there and started performing what he called 'manito magic' to bring out the spirits of the dead to defend their holy ground."

"We saw them," Bess said, sitting up and staring.

"We laughed at him," Mrs. Johnson continued. "We even ran him off the property several times, but he always came back. We couldn't police it twenty-four hours a day. Then we saw the ghosts. And everything started dying. This used to be a thriving community because we had lots of people come to the lake. Now everything's gone. The only reason I'm still here is that this is my home and I have nowhere else to go. Mr. Johnson passed away many years ago."

"Isn't that government property?" Nancy asked. "A state park, if I remember correctly?"

The woman nodded. "We had the government people come out," she said. "They saw the ghosts, too. But you can't put that on an official report."

"That must be why the road is still open," Nancy said. "No one could come up with an official reason for closing it."

"Sad but true," Mrs. Johnson said. "I suppose you'll be leaving in the morning?"

"Absolutely," Bess said.

"I'm not so sure," Nancy said. "This may be too good a mystery to let stand."

While Mrs. Johnson made dinner, the girls got ready for bed. When the woman returned, she brought with her not only the cheeseburgers but also a large bowl of salad and three slices of steaming homemade apple pie!

The young detectives ate ravenously. Nancy was far hungrier than she had realized. But she couldn't get the ghosts of Lake Oolagah out of her mind. As they finished the last of their pie, she determined that they would not leave the area until they had gotten to the bottom of the mystery.

Nancy awoke early from a restless sleep. She dressed quietly to avoid waking George and Bess, then slipped outside to make a phone call. By the time she returned to the cabin, the girls were awake.

"Are we really staying around this creepy place?" Bess asked as she combed her blonde hair.

Nancy perched on the end of the bed, looking fresh in her yellow shorts and blouse. "Well, we have to get the gear that you didn't want to take last night. It wouldn't hurt to poke around the lake a little while we're there."

"Does that mean yes or no?" George asked.

Nancy stood up. "It means, let's go down to the office and have a nice breakfast with Mrs. Johnson and see what the day brings."

Bess frowned at her reflection in the dresser mirror. "It means, we're staying."

An hour later, they were back on the secluded road to Lake Oolagah.

"This looks just as spooky in the daytime," George said.

Nancy's attention was caught by a cloud drifting overhead. It was a strange-looking cloud, brighter than any she had ever seen. She wondered what it was.

When the girls arrived at the spot where they had begun to set up camp the night before, they gasped.

"Our gear's gone!" George exclaimed.

"My dad's going to kill me!" cried Bess, thinking of the new Coleman stove and lantern she had borrowed.

"Don't worry," Nancy said. "I think I know where the equipment is."

"You do?" George stared at her.

"I do." Nancy smiled. "And this is the break I've been looking for."

Without another word, she turned the car around and headed back up the road, stopping near what she figured was John Bearcloud's shack.

"Come on," she said, getting out. "Let's meet the man who brought the curse to Lake Oolagah."

"You must be kidding!" Bess said. "Suppose he decides to have us for dinner or something?"

"We'll let him eat you first," George replied sardonically.

"Very funny," Bess said, and made a face.

As they moved through the bleak landscape to the

tumbledown shack, the strange white cloud was still drifting overhead. Nancy had an uneasy feeling about it, but she could not explain why.

They closed in on the shack. Its appearance was even more ragged when they came up close.

"There's our gear," George said, suddenly, pointing to a pile of camping equipment near the front door.

Just then, a large man wearing a plaid flannel shirt stepped out of the hut. His long black hair was tied back at the nape of his neck and his angular face was filled with deep creases. "What do you want?" he boomed.

"You must be John Bearcloud," Nancy said.

"What do you want?" the man demanded again.

"That's our gear," Nancy said, pointing to the stack. "We left it last night and came to get it."

"Why did you leave it?" he asked harshly.

"We saw the ghost lights and got scared," Bess said. "Please give us the stuff back. My father will be really mad it I don't bring it home."

"This is Indian land," Bearcloud declared. "Whites must stay away."

"Someone told us it belonged to the Delaware Indians," Nancy said, "but we didn't learn which tribe."

John Bearcloud just stared at her. "Leave," he said after a moment.

"What about our gear?" Bess persisted.

"Take it and go!"

"That cloud," Nancy said, pointing to the bright white nimbus. "What is that?"

147

Bearcloud barely glanced up. "The Manito," he said. "The Great Spirit protecting this land."

"You never told me what tribe is buried here," Nancy said.

"Cree Indian," he said. "Now go!"

The girls grabbed the equipment and retraced their steps through the woods. Bess was panting when they arrived at the car.

"Nancy Drew," she wheezed. "Why do you get us into these things. That man was frightening!"

"Well, now that you're acquainted," Nancy smiled, "you won't mind going back."

"What?" Bess looked dumbfounded.

Nancy got in the car and began pumping the gas pedal.

"What are you doing?" George asked.

"Flooding the engine," Nancy replied.

"But then we won't be able to leave!" Bess protested.

Nancy nodded. "That's the idea."

After pumping the pedal for several moments, she tried to start the car. It whined loudly, but wouldn't turn over.

"Do you think John Bearcloud can hear this in his shack?" she asked George over the noise of the crying engine.

"Sure," George replied. "But why are you doing this?"

"I want him over here helping with the car so I can check out his shack," Nancy said.

"What do you expect to find in there?"

149

Nancy shrugged. "I won't know until I look."

She climbed out of the car. "Go up and ask him for help," she said. "I won't need any more than five or ten minutes." She disappeared between the trees. Bess looked unhappy. "Do we have to?" she murmured. Then she got out reluctantly.

From a distance, Nancy watched her friends approach the shack. There were many large rocks in the woods, and she kept out of sight hiding behind one of them.

Finally, she heard Bearcloud's voice loudly telling the girls he knew nothing about cars. But George insisted and finally persuaded him to take a look. Nancy watched them walk past her vantage point, then ran to the shack when it was safe.

The front door was open and she slipped inside. It was a dismal place, containing one small table with a lantern on it, a sleeping bag on the floor, and a tiny dresser made of unfinished wood.

On the table lay a savings book. She opened it to find John Bearcloud had an account of twenty-five thousand dollars!

Putting the bank book back on the table, Nancy moved to the dresser and pulled out the drawers. The first contained canned goods. In the second were clothes, mostly jeans and flannel shirts. The third drawer was filled with hundreds of clear plastic trashbags and candles. The bags were large, industrial ones, and had D.E. printed on them in red letters.

All at once, Nancy heard the Indian's voice coming closer.

"I don't care *how* you get it out," he said. "Just leave!"

She quickly closed the drawers and looked around. If she went out the front door, he would see her! Turning, she noticed a place where the uneven boards had been cut through for ventilation to the outside.

She ran to the makeshift window and squeezed through it just as the Indian came through the door!

There was a gully behind the shack. Nancy scurried to it and jumped down to hide. When she was sure it was safe, she walked along the gully away from the house, then moved through the woods to join her friends, who were already in the car.

"We were afraid he'd caught you!" George cried in relief.

"You were supposed to keep him here until I was finished!" Nancy said, climbing into the driver's seat.

"He wouldn't stay," Bess said. "I think he suspected something. He kept asking where you were."

Nancy turned the ignition without pumping the gas pedal. The car whined for several seconds, then roared to life. She drove off.

"Did you find what you were looking for?" George asked.

"I don't know," Nancy said, and described what she had discovered in the shack.

"That's a lot of money for someone who lives out in the woods," Bess said. "That seems suspicious."

"Not necessarily," Nancy said. "Where John Bearcloud chooses to live is his own business. John Paul Getty was one of the richest men in the world, yet he

151

rode to work on the bus and brought his lunch in a paper bag. Right now, I'm more interested in the things I found in the drawer."

"The candles and trashbags?" George asked.

"Anyone who doesn't have garbage pickup and electricity would have those things," Bess pointed out.

"But he had so many," Nancy said. "Also, the trashbags were industrial ones, not the kind you buy in the supermarket."

"Maybe he has a friend who works for a company that makes them," Bess said.

Nancy passed the road they had turned down by mistake the night before and suddenly stepped on the brakes. "D.E.!" she exclaimed. "That's it."

"What's it?" George looked dumbfounded.

"The D.E. that was printed on the garbage bags stands for Dunbar Enterprises!" Nancy responded excitedly.

She checked the road behind her, then backed up and took the road to the factory.

"Where are we going?" Bess inquired.

"I want to look at the company again," Nancy explained. She stopped the car about twenty yards away from the guard station, prompting the day-shift guard to walk out and stare at them.

"That's no cloud at all," Nancy said to her friends, pointing to the bright white fluff overhead. "Bearcloud called it Manito, but it's smoke, and it's coming from that odd-shaped building over there."

She indicated a structure that looked like a large

cylinder squeezed together in the middle and bulging out at the top and bottom.

"What's this got to do with anything?" Bess asked.

"I'm not sure," Nancy said, "but I bet there's a link between Bearcloud, Dunbar Enterprises and the death of Lake Oolagah," Nancy declared, and turned the car around to drive back to the motel.

Mrs. Johnson was waving to them from the office door when they pulled into the parking lot.

"Nancy Drew!" she called when they had parked. "Your father phoned while you were gone."

"Oh, good," Nancy returned. "He must have something to tell me."

"How did your dad know we were here?" George asked.

"I called him this morning while you were still asleep," Nancy told her. "I asked him to check on a few things for me. Go on down to the room. I'll join you after I've returned his call."

When Nancy phoned her father, he *did* have news for her.

"You were right about the Delaware Indians," he said. "They were a loose confederation of what are known as the Algonkin tribes that traveled the hunting trails in the Northeastern United States and Southern Canada."

"Could they have come this far South?" Nancy asked.

"It's not impossible," her father returned. "But remember, they were nomadic wanderers who spent

153

much of their time on the trail. They would have no set burial ground."

"That's what I wanted to know!" Nancy exclaimed. "Thanks, Dad. What about Dunbar Enterprises?"

"I checked with the Environmental Protection Agency on Dunbar's Cleveland plant. The reason it moved to Lake Oolagah is that it was in trouble with the EPA over pollution."

"Pollution?"

"That's right. There is dangerous waste connected with the making of plastics, and Dunbar Enterprises was dumping this waste into the Ohio River. When the company was caught, the owners claimed their plant had been built many years before the environmental standards had been established."

He paused a moment, then went on. "The EPA told Dunbar no charges would be pressed if he built a new, safer plant. Apparently he did, near Lutherville. When it was finished, the EPA approved it as far as pollution emissions were concerned."

"Sounds as if I've run into a dead end on that one," Nancy said. After a few more moments, she said good-bye to her father and hung up.

She was confused. The damage to the lake had begun right after Dunbar Enterprises had moved into the area. Yet, its EPA monitoring proved that wastes were properly disposed of.

She walked to the cabin, where Mrs. Johnson was putting new linen on her bed. As Nancy watched the woman flick her wrist and snap the sheet out to let it float gently down onto the mattress, she had a thought.

"That's it!" she cried out.

"What's it?" George stopped brushing her hair in midair and stared at her.

"I have a plan," Nancy said, and quickly explained her idea to her friends and their pleasant hostess.

There was no moonlight that night when the three young detectives parked near the turnoff path to the lake. Nancy turned the headlights off.

"Now we wait," she said.

"I hear someone coming!" George said after about ten minutes. A moment later, the girls saw headlights bumping slowly along the road.

A white Dunbar truck passed them without seeing their car and disappeared in the direction of the lake.

"What'll we do now?" George asked.

"I'll drop you off before we get to the lake," Nancy said. "Go to Bearcloud's cabin. He shouldn't be there. Grab the candles and bags and come down to the lake, okay?"

George sighed. "Okay."

After letting her friends out of the car, Nancy continued to the lake. When she came to the spillway, the Dunbar truck was already backed up and a man in a protective white suit opened a valve protruding from its rear. John Bearcloud stood next to him, watching.

When the Indian saw Nancy, he ran toward her, his face contorted with anger. "Get out of here!" he roared.

Instead, Nancy stepped out of her car and went up to

the truck. "I wouldn't do that if I were you," she said.

The man in the white suit stared at her. "I'm just dumping septic tank water in the lake," he said.

"Water it may be," Nancy said. "But it contains radioactive waste!"

"What?"

"Get out!" Bearcloud screamed again. He tried to grab her arm, but she sidestepped nimbly.

"I figured out your scheme," she told him calmly, even though she was shaking inside. "The Delaware Indians were wanderers; they never had burial grounds. I also checked with the EPA on Dunbar Enterprises. They gave the company a clean bill, but I saw that white cloud coming out of the odd-shaped building next to the Dunbar plant. It made me wonder."

Bearcloud stared at her, his mouth open. "So?" he finally prodded, unsure what to do.

"It occurred to me that the building might be the cooling tower for a small nuclear reactor," Nancy went on, "which provides the electricity for Dunbar. It also produces nuclear waste that must be disposed of. Reactors are not checked by the EPA. It would be up to the NRC, the Nuclear Regulatory Commission."

"Listen, kid!" Bearcloud fumed. "You just turn around and forget you saw anything if you know what's good for you." He stepped up to Nancy once more, his hands outstretched.

"Look!" the man in white shouted all of a sudden.

Ghost lights were moving through the woods, lots and lots of them!

"What's going on?" the Indian screamed.

"I'm getting out of here," the man in the white suit yelled and jumped into his truck. But Nancy's car was blocking the road!

He got out and ran up to Nancy. "Give me the key!" he ordered.

She pulled it out of her pocket and threw it in the lake!

"You—" the driver began when a voice called out from behind them. "Hold it!"

A man in a blue suit flanked by two police officers walked up to the group. "I'm George Macklin from the Nuclear Energy Commission," he introduced himself. He turned to the truck driver and Bearcloud. "You two are under arrest for dumping radioactive waste into Lake Oolagah!"

"I had nothing to do with this!" Bearcloud protested.

"Wrong!" George cried out. She and Bess had just come from his cabin with trashbags and candles under their arms. "You've been making ghost lights and scaring away the local people to cover this up. And Dunbar payed you plenty for your services."

"I don't know what you're talking about," the Indian said.

Bess tied a lighted candle into the opening of one of the plastic bags. "Like this," she said. "We set off a few before we came. It works very well." The hot air from the candle filled the bag and it rose from the ground floating upwards.

George Macklin smiled at Nancy. "When you called

me this afternoon," he said, "I had my doubts. But you were absolutely right. Dunbar dumped wastes into the lake and killed everything in it and around it!" He congratulated the girls for their good work, then drove the officers and the two prisoners to the local police station.

After they had left, Nancy turned to her friends. "Now we have another mystery to solve," she said with a twinkle in her eyes.

"What's that?" Bess demanded.

"How to get out of here. I had to throw my keys in the lake, or that truck driver would have taken them."

"Oh, no!" George groaned and both she and Bess sank to the ground and covered their faces.

Nancy giggled. "I'm only kidding. I have a spare key under the front seat!"